The Grumpy (

I am a grumpy old author. I grew up partly at Mercury Bay on the Coromandel Peninsula. All we ever seemed to do was camp, fish, swim, sail, row, dig for gold, collect kauri gum, and go on picnics. Around the camp-fires, and lying in our sacking bunks at night, we listened to our mother and aunts and uncles talk about the time when they were children. All they ever seemed to do was to camp, fish, swim, sail, row, dig for gold, chop down kauri trees, and go for picnics. And listen to their mother and father telling stories of Home, a foreign land around the other side of the world.

Back in those Mercury Bay days, there was no school. Summer lasted for ever. It never rained, and the sun shone all the time so we could go on picnics every day. The tide was always high, and the water warm for swimming. We didn't need money because we lived on fish, wild pigs, mussels, pipis, oysters, and crayfish. We raided orchards, ate too many green plums and apples, and had terrible stomach-aches.

We thought that wonderful life was going to go on for ever. But we grew up. I've been grumpy ever since. The next best thing to being young in the 1930s is to write about it. That's why I wrote *Aunt Effie*.

We had an aunt who loved the sea and always owned a boat, who took us on picnics, and who caught more fish than the rest of us put together. She also wore slacks, smoked, and drank beer, which some people said was wicked. We wanted to be wicked, too. We admired and loved our aunt. This book is dedicated to her memory.

—Jack Lasenby

Also by Jack Lasenby

Aunt Effie

Jack Lasenby

"Yo-ho-ho, and a bottle of Old Puckeroo!"

With illustrations by David Elliot

Longacre Press

Published with the assistance of
ARTS COUNCIL OF NEW ZEALAND *TOI AOTEAROA*

Jack Lasenby asserts his moral right to be identified as the
author of this work.

© Jack Lasenby

ISBN 1 877135 72 0

First published by Longacre Press 2002,
9 Dowling Street, Dunedin, New Zealand.

Book and cover design by Christine Buess
Cover illustration and book illustrations by David Elliot
Printed by McPherson's Printing Group

Contents

To the memory of Aunty Marge

Chapter One

How Nelson's Column Got its Name

Our Aunt Effie adored being ill. Best of all she liked colds, flu, and the collywobbles she got after eating green apples. Real illnesses she ignored until they gave up and sneaked away, but a runny nose, a stubbed toe, or a pimple, and she popped on her heavy green canvas invalid's pyjamas, jumped into bed, and bellowed for her nephews and nieces. And, since she could never re-member which one of us was which, she called all our names.

"Daisy-Mabel-Johnny-Flossie-Lynda-Stan-Howard-Marge-Stuart!" she shouted. "Peter-Marie-Colleen-Alwyn-Bryce-Jack!" she bawled. "Ann-Jazz-Becky-Jane-Isaac-David-Victor! Casey-Lizzie-Jared-Jess!" We dropped our milking buckets, cake mixtures, axes, scythes, curry-combs, scrubbing brushes, whips, needles, shovels, and shears and ran up the stairs.

Aunt Effie lay on a pile of pillows, a sou'wester tied under her chin, an oilskin coat around her shoulders, her feet on a stone hot-water bottle. "I'm cold," she shivered. "Stir up the fire!"

Marie struck sparks from the flint and steel Aunt Effie kept on the mantelpiece. As the tinder smoked, she blew on it till flames licked the dry tea-tree twigs we used for kindling. She fed on bigger sticks and branches, and the backlog that had been smouldering began to glow. Wind grumbled in the chimney. The firelight made the shadows even darker under Aunt Effie's enormous bed, and we clutched each other as something there moved.

The flames flickered and reflected off hilts and triggers on the walls. Great cupboards, presses, and chests of drawers stepped forward into the light. Later, the flames died down, and the furniture stepped back into the dark amongst tall mirrors, a dented suit of armour with a bullet-hole through the helmet, and a blunderbuss. A musket and a cutlass hung on the back of a chair. A pike, a halberd, and an ancient banner leaned in a corner. Sometimes we could see the pike had something stuck on it, something with long hair....

A cannon stuck its ugly mouth out the window, and a tidy pyramid of cannon-balls stood beside it. Where most people had the handle of a chamber pot sticking out from under their bed, Aunt Effie had a tarred barrel with a drawing of a skull and crossbones. Daisy, who disapproved of strong drink, said the barrel was filled with rum, but Peter said it was just gunpowder for the cannon. None of us dared look because of the thing that moved in the shadows under the bed.

Stags' heads, buffaloes, lions, elephants, dinosaurs,

snakes, crocodiles, tigers, boars, and leopards watched us from the walls, their eyes winking and glinting. We knew they were really alive and just stuck their heads through holes in the wall – because they often changed places. Skeletons of a shark, a swordfish, and a killer whale hung from the ceiling. Stuffed trout as big as kangaroos swam through the gloom overhead.

"Come on, Peter-Marie-Colleen-Alwyn-Bryce-Jack, they won't eat you!" Aunt Effie said. "Jump up, Ann-Jazz-Becky-Jane-Isaac-David-Victor," she exclaimed as we climbed on to the foot of her enormous bed. "Are you comfortable, Casey-Lizzie-Jared-Jessie?

"If you haven't enough room, shove the dogs out of the way. Caligula-Nero-Brutus-Kaiser-Genghis-Boris, move over and make room for the kids!" The dogs bared their teeth and growled like gravel boiling in a pot. They scared Daisy who was self-righteous and knew the Bible backwards. Alwyn, who could never walk past a paddock without bellowing at the bull, nor past a dog without barking at it, climbed on to the bed, and the dogs looked surly but moved over for him. The rest of us followed. There was room for everyone on Aunt Effie's enormous bed.

Once we were settled, propped against each other or sprawling lost among eiderdowns, Aunt Effie would groan, "I am dying, Egypt, dying!" She'd reach for a bottle of Old Puckeroo Smelling Salts, pull out the cork with her teeth, take a swig, and sit up straight, hair on end.

Lizzie once asked, "Why do you drink smelling salts,

9

Aunt Effie?" But Aunt Effie didn't hear because of the smoke still coming out her ears as she smacked the cork back in, stuck the bottle under her pillow, and asked, "Do you know how Nelson's Column got its name?"

We chorused, "No! Tell us?" and snuggled down among the blankets, eiderdowns, dogs, and empty medicine bottles.

"Long before you were born," said Aunt Effie, "Captain Cook bumped into an enormous tree floating off Cape Horn. He towed it behind the *Endeavour* back to England and up the Thames to London. 'It's proof,' he declared, 'of an unknown land in the South Pacific!' The Lord Mayor planted the tree in the middle of London, and German and Japanese tourists came in thousands to take photographs and carve their names on it.

"Now, Admiral Nelson had just thrashed Napoleon at the Battle of Timbuktu, and Queen Victorious showed how grateful she was by making him a lord and casting a statue of him. She called for a volunteer to climb the tree and bolt the statue on top. I was just a girl at the time, but I stuffed my crinoline into the legs of my bloomers and shinned up. It took me several weeks, the tree was so tall. I couldn't see much of England because of the clouds below, but over their white bulges I could see the Mediterranean, the Pillars of Hercules, and – just over the edge of the world – the beginning of Africa."

"What's the edge of the world?" Lizzie asked.

"Those nutters at school will tell you the world is round," said Aunt Effie, "but anyone in their right mind can see it's flat. The world is a box with six flat sides," she said. "When you get to the end of one side, you sail over the edge and across the next side – if you're lucky."

"What if you're unlucky?"

"You fall into space!" Aunt Effie snapped her teeth, and we crawled towards the middle of her bed.

"One side of the world is Britain, Europe, and the Mediterranean," said Aunty Effie. "The next side is Africa and India. Another side's Russia, China, and the North Pole. North and South America are another side. The fifth side is Australia and Japan. If you keep going long enough – without falling into space – you come to the South Pacific with our country and the South Pole. We're on the opposite side of the box from Britain, which is why Poms all have flat heads from walking on them."

"If the world's shaped like a box, what's inside it?" Jessie asked Aunt Effie, who pretended not to hear. Jessie changed her question. "Did you bolt Admiral Nelson's statue on top?"

"Maybe this will give you some idea of the height of that giant tree. It took so long to pull the statue up that, by the time I got it to the top, it had gone bald. Instead of looking like Admiral Nelson it had turned into Julius Caesar. Anyway, I bolted it into place, and the Londoners have called the giant tree Nelson's Column ever since. They don't use their eyes, Londoners. Of course Queen Victorious was so short she couldn't tell the difference.

"She gave me a golden sword with a whacking great ruby for my trouble. They're somewhere over there." We looked and saw a flash of red and a flicker of gold in the shadows.

"Since I was a good climber, Queen Victorious asked me to stay in Buckingham Palace and appointed me her Royal Chimney-Sweep, but I wanted to find the unknown land where that giant tree grew. Queen Victorious thought I was ungrateful. 'Off with her head!' she said to the executioner. While he was sharpening his axe, I cut off my hair, knitted it into a false beard, and stowed away on a ship bound for the Pacific.

"The bosun found me hidden among the cable tiers, the thirtieth day out. I'd had nothing to eat but my false beard, so they gave me a bottle of rum and a ship's biscuit full of weevils. Then the captain ordered me to be fired out of a cannon.

"'That's not fair!' I told him.

"'I don't care whether it's fair or not!' Captain Flash shrieked and jumped on top of a barrel to get away from the rats gnawing at his feet. 'I'm not wasting good rum and weevils on a stowaway.' He shrieked again as a big rat put its paws on top of the barrel and went to climb up beside him. I saw at a glance that Captain Flash was a coward.

"I wrung the big rat's neck and wrestled a couple of others to death. The cowardly captain jumped off the barrel, blew out his chest, and signed me on as the Ship's Rat-Catcher."

Aunt Effie took another swig of smelling salts and plumped up her pillows. "Each day," she said, "I crawled through the ship's bilges, a cutlass between my teeth and a pair of pistols in each hand, fighting the giant rats that had lived down there undisturbed for centuries.

Old rats with grey beards down to their chests, and tusks so long they'd grown in circles. I slit their throats and swayed them up on deck where Captain Flash kicked their carcasses overboard and sank them with cannon fire.

"Oh, yes!" Aunt Effie grinned, "he was very brave once they were dead.

"There was one rat the size of an old horse, hairless and bald, and his name was Herodotus. He was the father of liars and told some good yarns, and I fed him cheese and rum. We became friends.

"Halfway between Africa and Australia, Captain Flash thought his ship was clear of rats. 'There's nothing left for a rat-catcher to do,' he told me. 'Besides, you're starting to look a bit like a girl, and girls are hoodoos at sea. I think we might throw you overboard.'"

"'Herodotus!' I called. A huge grey paw shoved aside the hatch cover. It scrumbled across the deck, feeling for the captain, its great claws digging lumps out of the planks. Captain Flash screeched, fell on his knees, and prayed to be forgiven.

"'Down, boy!' I called, and Herodotus' huge paw slid down the hatch and out of sight like a grey boulder.

"There was no more talk of hoodoos and throwing me overboard." Aunt Effie shook the bottle of Old Puckeroo Smelling Salts beside her ear, and flung it under the bed where it rolled and clinked against something. Her voice slurred: "I think I'll just have a little zizz."

"Did you find the land of the giant tree?" Lizzie asked.

There was no reply, just a snore from Aunt Effie.

We went to slide down to the floor, but a big gruff voice said, "Watch out for the Bugaboo!" and we all shrieked and clasped each other. We knew the Bugaboo hid under Aunt Effie's enormous bed waiting to catch us by the foot and eat us.

We pushed and shoved the four little ones to the edge. They fought back, nobody wanting to be first, until the smallest, Jessie, fell over the side. She got up crying and ran for the door, and we jumped as far as we could and ran downstairs after her, shrieking, giggling, not daring to look back where Aunt Effie lay smiling to herself, snoring and sweating in her heavy green canvas pyjamas.

Note: *"Aunt Effie has no right telling us stories full of difficult words that the little ones don't understand. I must ask her what are cable tiers, weevils, and hoodoos. I just want to help the little ones, of course."* —Daisy.

Chapter Two

Captain Flash and his Ear-Trumpet

"*Daisy-Mabel*-Johnny-Flossie-Lynda-Stan-Howard-Marge-Stuart! Peter-Marie-Colleen-Alwyn-Bryce-Jack! Ann-Jazz-Becky-Jane-Isaac-David-Victor! Casey-Lizzie-Jared-Jess!" Aunt Effie called in her strong voice. We ran up the stairs and leapt on to the foot of her enormous bed. The dogs wouldn't shift, but we snarled back until they made room for all of us except Daisy who had to perch on a bedpost.

Aunt Effie sat up against her pillows in her heavy green canvas invalid's pyjamas, looking at a map. She rolled it up, took her false teeth out of a glass of water, popped them in, and chewed. The false teeth made a noise like billiard balls knocking.

"I told you we were sailing between Africa and Australia," Aunt Effie said, "looking for the land of the giant tree, when the ancient rat, Herodotus, saved me from being flung over the side in a barrel.

"We were wrecked in the middle of the Indian Ocean,

15

all because of Captain Flash's incompetence. Ah!" Aunt Effie sighed, "I could have loved that man...."

"You said he tried to fire you out of a cannon," Daisy reminded her.

"So he did," said Aunt Effie. "A coward and an incompetent Captain Flash might have been, but he was both amorous and an excellent dancer. Many a hornpipe we danced on the quarterdeck during those moonlit nights as we sailed across the Indian Ocean. Captain Flash looked so fetching in his best uniform, medals jingling on his chest, silver spurs ringing on his heels, gold epaulettes clashing on his shoulders, and the ends of his long moustaches getting caught in the rigging. Unfortunately he was deaf from firing people out of the cannons and had to use a big brass ear-trumpet. How could I respect a man with a trumpet stuck in his ear?"

"Hmph!" said Daisy and gave a howl. Boris had bitten her.

"Don't go teasing the dogs, Daisy-Mabel-Johnny-Flossie-Lynda-Stan-Howard-Marge-Stuart," Aunt Effie said. "Well, Captain Flash was dancing with me on the quarterdeck, one night, when he should have been looking where the ship was going. So he could bow to me, he'd stuck his ear-trumpet on top of his head like a pointed helmet. There was a crash and a bump as the ship ran on to a coral island. A snatch-block fell from the mizzen-mast and drove the ear-trumpet down over his head as far as his shoulders.

"Most of the crew panicked and jumped into the shark-infested waters. As the ship sank I took Captain

Flash's hand and led him aboard a raft. The carpenter followed with his chest of tools, the cook with his pots and pans, the ship's blacksmith carrying his forge, hammers, and tongs, and an impertinent cabin boy. The only sounds were the munching of sharks, the screams of the unfortunate crew, and the tinny creak of Captain Flash yelling inside his ear-trumpet.

"Safe on the coral island, the carpenter built a sailing gig. The blacksmith drilled eyeholes, nostrils, and a mouth-hole through the ear-trumpet for Captain Flash. The impertinent cabin boy sewed a sail."

"What's impertinent?" asked Lizzie.

"Listen," Aunt Effie told her, "and you'll find out.

"Next morning, the beach was littered with wooden legs that had washed ashore: all that remained of the unhappy crew. The carpenter made a mast out of them and a spar for our dipping lugsail."

"What's a dipping lugsail?" asked Daisy.

"When you come about," said Aunt Effie, "to go on another tack, a lugsail dips around the mast. If you don't dip your head, you get clouted around the ears. That's why it's called a dipping lugsail." Aunt Effie stared fiercely at our oldest cousin. "Any other stupid questions?" she demanded, but we were all silent except for Daisy who was still rubbing her leg where Boris had bitten it.

Aunt Effie pulled out a bottle. "Rub a bit of this on." Daisy took one look at the bottle and felt better at once. "Old Puckeroo Strong Liniment for Cuts and Abrasions," said Auntie Effie and took a swig before smacking the cork back in the bottle and stuffing it under her pillow.

"We had sailed away from the coral island," she said, "when the impertinent cabin boy complained, 'This gig's slow. And it's getting smaller.' It was quite comfortable until he said that. Then, to make things worse, he said, 'It's only big enough for five people.' If only he'd kept his mouth shut," sighed Auntie Effie, "we'd never have noticed there were seats only for five.

"One of us had to go. The cook stewed the wretched boy, and we ate him. The gig now fitted us admirably: the cook, the carpenter, the blacksmith, Captain Flash, and me."

We stared at Aunt Effie. Jessie and Jared crawled away as far as they could without falling off the end of her enormous bed. Boris and Kaiser watched and showed their teeth in a nasty grin.

"After a few more days in the water, the gig seemed to shrink," said Aunt Effie. "Either that, or we'd all got fat from eating the cabin boy. 'This boat's slow because it's only big enough for four,' said the cook, one morning. He left us no choice," said Aunt Effie. "He was fat, as cooks often are, so he lasted a fair way across the Indian Ocean. We were in sight of Australia before we finished eating him."

Looking over their shoulders at Aunt Effie, Lizzie and Casey crawled after Jared and Jessie. Boris and Kaiser smacked their lips and ground their teeth at them.

"I should have said," Aunt Effie added, "we made the cook tell us all his recipes before we ate him. The gig fitted the four of us admirably: the carpenter, the blacksmith, Captain Flash with his head stuck inside his ear-trumpet, and me."

"What do people taste like?" asked one of our older cousins.

"Rather like pork without the crackling," said Aunt Effie. "I do like a nice bit of crackling – with apple sauce." She looked at the cousin who had asked the question, leaned forward, and prodded him with her long finger. "You've got a nice bit of fat on you, Peter-Marie-Colleen-Alwyn-Bryce-Jack...." Auntie Effie smacked her lips. Our cousin hid amongst the eiderdowns and didn't ask any more questions.

"As we left Australia behind and sailed around the next corner and over the edge of the world, the blacksmith sneezed," said Aunt Effie. "A fastidious man – just for one moment he let go of the rope that held him in and wiped his nose. Before he could stick his hanky back in his pocket and grab the rope again, he fell into space, dwindling rapidly to a shrieking black dot. I was grateful he'd already shown me how the forge worked. It was surprising how comfortable the gig was, now there were only three of us, the carpenter, Captain Flash, and me.

"Once you've sailed around the corner from Australia, and over the edge of the world, the Tasman Sea is so flat that the smallest wind blows up large waves. One was so high, it took us six months to sail up its front, and another six to sail down its back. Captain Flash was seasick inside his ear-trumpet, and the carpenter, who really should have known better, said, 'I think the gig's sailing slower because it's getting smaller.'

"He had already shown me how to use his chest of tools so, after Captain Flash and I had eaten the carpenter, I lengthened the gig, put up a mast aft, and schooner-rigged the ship.

"I leaned over the stern and called, 'You can come aboard now,' and my friend, Herodotus, the enormous rat, clambered out of the water. He'd been hanging on to the transom with one hand all the way from the coral island and chewing the gig a little shorter each night. Since sailing speed is a function of length, that was why we'd got slower, but it was too late to tell that to the cabin boy, the cook, the blacksmith, and the carpenter.

"We soon saw land in the distance, but Captain Flash kept complaining. 'There seems to be something else in the boat with us,' he said. 'Something grey and enormous.' Fortunately he couldn't see very well through the eyeholes the blacksmith had drilled in his ear-trumpet.

"'You're imagining things,' I told him comfortably.

"'Are you quite sure?' he asked.

"'Would I lie to you?'

"Captain Flash made a strange sound inside his ear-trumpet.

"Herodotus winked at me and, although I shook my head, he blew on the back of Captain Flash's neck, just where the ear-trumpet came down to his shoulders.

"Captain Flash screamed. 'Something blew on the back of my neck!' Herodotus grinned and sat back, whiskers twitching.

"'A breeze has sprung up,' I told Captain Flash. 'It won't be long now before we reach land.'

"'I hope there's somebody there who can cut this ear-trumpet off my head,' said Captain Flash. 'I must look such a fool!'

"'Not at all!' I assured him, and Herodotus sat shaking with silent laughter and pointing at the Captain. Just then I saw something on the horizon: giant trees sticking out of the sea. "'Land ahoy!' I shouted!"

Aunt Effie sat up in bed, her sou'wester falling over her eyes. "Land ahoy!" She shouted so loud she blew us all off the end of her enormous bed, down the stairs, and out into the orchard. We didn't even have time to be scared of the Bugaboo.

Note: "*Epaulettes, snatch-block, mizzen-mast, lugsail, schooner! How can Aunt Effie expect the little ones to understand such difficult words?*" —Daisy.

Chapter Three

The Scarf and the
Amazing Timber-Jack

"*Daisy-Mabel*-Johnny-Flossie-Lynda-Stan-Howard-Marge-Stuart! Marie-Peter-Colleen-Alwyn-Bryce-Jack! Ann-Jazz-Becky-Jane-Isaac-David-Victor! Casey-Lizzie-Jared-Jess!"

We just had time to run upstairs and make ourselves comfortable on the foot of Aunt Effie's enormous bed before she went on with her story.

"The giant trees sticking out of the sea were even bigger than the one Captain Cook towed to London," she said. "The whole of the new land was flattened under their weight. Of course, once the trees were cut down, it bounced up into hills and mountains. It still shakes itself around occasionally, what people who don't know any better call earthquakes.

"I asked Captain Flash what name we should give the country we had discovered, and he said, 'Aotearoa,' which was the name of Queen Victorious's favourite husband."

"Did she have more than one husband?" asked Casey.

"Queens had dozens of husbands in those days! Anyway, I didn't think much of Aotearoa as a name for our country, so I said to Captain Flash I couldn't hear him properly.

"I left him shouting inside the ear-trumpet and ran up the rigging. From the mast-head, I could see the land squashed flat under the enormous trees. And I could also see it already had a perfectly good name painted along its side: Waharoa!

"This country not only had a perfectly good name already, but it had a perfectly good painter, Colin McCahon, who painted the names on everything so people wouldn't forget them. He painted 'Waharoa' along the side of the country. He painted 'Kauri' on the giant trees, 'Maori' on the Maoris, and 'Pakeha' on the Pakehas. It's such a comfort," Aunt Effie sighed, "to know everything's got its proper name. You take Australia, they don't know whether they're Arthur or Martha over there because they didn't have a painter like Colin McCahon. I've often thought," she said, "it would be easier if I painted your names on you. It would save me time."

But we cried and said we liked her calling out all our names.

"The giant kauris grew so close together," said Aunt Effie, "there was no room for us to step ashore. I had to scarf the first kauri tree while standing on Herodotus' back in the gig. And the trouble we had putting in the back-cut!"

"What's the scarf?" asked Lizzie.

"What's the back-cut?" asked Jessie.

Aunt Effie stared at them. "When you've cut the scarf, you chip off the bark around the tree and start sawing from the other side – what you call the back-cut."

"Why chip off the bark?" Lizzie asked.

Aunt Effie stared again. "We pitched a tent over the enormous stump and I danced a hornpipe with Captain Flash while Herodotus played the music on our cross-cut saw."

"How do you play music on a saw?"

"You bend it and play up and down the back of it with a bow – like playing the fiddle," said Aunt Effie. "It has a languishing tone that reduces its hearers to tears, the musical saw. Herodotus played while the Captain wept and danced. He made such a dashing figure despite the polished brass ear-trumpet jammed over his head, I could have fallen in love with him, even though I knew he was both a coward and an incompetent."

Aunt Effie tore off a strip of her heavy green canvas invalid's pyjamas, wiped her eyes, and blew her nose like a bugle.

"Herodotus and the Captain sawed the trunk into logs, but they were still too big to move, so I invented the timber-jack."

"What's a timber-jack?"

"You can't believe its power. 'Give me a place to stand, and I'll move the world with my timber-jack!' Herodotus used to say."

"What did it look like?" Jessie wanted to know.

Aunt Effie glanced and saw Lizzie was about to ask

another question. She sighed. "Perhaps we'd better go and chop down a tree ourselves. Then you'll see what a scarf is, why saws jam, and what's a timber-jack.

"Here," she said, taking a green envelope from under her pillow. "Run and shake this on the fire, Daisy-Mabel-Johnny-Flossie-Lynda-Stan-Howard-Marge-Stuart-Marie-Peter-Colleen-Alwyn-Bryce-Jack-Ann-Jazz-Becky-Jane-Isaac-David-Victor-Casey-Lizzie-Jared-Jessie, but jump back as quick as you can."

Lizzie shook the envelope so green powder spilled on the fire, and jumped back on the bed.

Whoof! The fireplace filled with green light, the room with green smoke. "Hold your noses!" shouted Aunt Effie. Green smoke whirled around us, green branches, green leaves, then green light dazzled, and we were standing holding our noses at the foot of the biggest tree we had ever seen. Everywhere we looked there were the huge grey columns of trees. Thick. Straight. We tipped back our heads and saw they had branches – high up – branches as thick through as ordinary-sized trees. They held up the sky.

"You can let go your noses now," said Aunt Effie. "Cut the scarf this side, the way we want it to fall."

Peter stood one side of the trunk and started chopping, and Marie started from the other side. When they got tired, the rest of us took it in turn. We chopped until a notch had been cut: almost flat on the bottom and slanting down on top. It was big enough for us to stand in, the scarf, but the kauri stood unmoved as we gnawed at its foot like mice.

"This is a twelve-foot, drag-tooth, cross-cut saw." Aunt Effie started Lizzie and Jessie sawing at the back of the kauri.

"It's stuck," said Lizzie.

"Ah!" said Aunt Effie.

"I think it's the bark getting stuck in the teeth," said Jessie.

"Ah!"

We chipped the bark away around the tree, where the back-cut was to go. Lizzie and Jessie got tired, so Casey and David had a go, and Jared and Victor. The saw ate into the trunk. Sawdust sprayed out either side. Then we found the trunk was so wide we couldn't pull the saw backwards and forwards without knocking our knuckles.

"What should we do?" asked Aunt Effie.

"Side-scarfs?" said Peter.

Aunt Effie nodded. Peter and Marie began chopping a scarf one side. Colleen and Alwyn started on the other side. They chopped and chopped and chopped. When they got tired, we all took turns. The side-scarfs weren't nearly as big as the first scarf, but we tried and found the saw would go back and forth again.

"It's too hard to pull."

"Then you need more people on the saw."

We tied a rope each end. Half of us pulled one way, half the other. The sawdust flew this way and that. Then the saw began to jam again.

"I think the tree's sitting on it," said Jazz.

Aunt Effie nodded.

"Is that what these are for?" Jazz asked.

"Try them," said Aunt Effie.

Jazz tapped a wedge into the back-cut. He swung a maul and drove it in. He hammered in a second wedge, and the saw moved freely again.

None of us can remember how long we sawed. Several days, or several weeks, or several months. Jared thought it was several years, "Because we all looked much older afterwards."

The sawing finished, the tree stood there still, so thick through it wouldn't fall over. Ann and Becky swung the mauls and drove in wedges on top of wedges in the back-cut. One day, the giant kauri leaned so the world seemed to slant. Into the gap made by the scarf, the tree fell and dragged down the sky. Where it had stood, the air rushed in so fast that lightning flashed and thunder boomed.

And the giant tree was still just beginning to fall.

A huge wind knocked us over. As fast as we climbed on our feet, it knocked us down again. Little branches, leaves, flakes of bark, and bits of kauri gum showered and pattered on us. The tree was so tall, it took several weeks after the bottom end hit the ground before the head smashed down, driving branches deep into the earth. It hit so hard, the country shook for hours, and we all kept falling over until it stopped bucking up and down. We looked at the devastation and cried.

We climbed on the stump and drove our axes side by side into the heart. We twitched the handles, snapped them off. And we took the mauls and drove the axes flush with the top of the stump. "Respect for the tree," Aunt Effie called it. So if you ever see a kauri stump, and in the middle of the stump you see red flakes of rust, you'll know it's the kauri we cut down.

We walked along the trunk of the fallen tree to the first branch. It took two months, Peter said, and we knew he must be right because he was the only one with a watch. We made ladders, climbed down and walked around the fallen head, smelling the raw earth tossed up, the smashed branches. We sniffed and bit the hard green cones that lay everywhere, we licked and tasted the lumps of kauri gum. We walked right around the head, climbed on top of the trunk, and began the long walk back to the stump. We looked at each other and looked away again. Nobody spoke.

We sawed the trunk into logs that lay like dead elephants through the bush. Then one of them came to life. We all stared as the front end tilted, and it slid down-hill into the creek bed. Where the log had been, Aunt Effie spun the double-handle on a shaft of wood half as high as herself. Steel toes stood out its bottom end. And a toothed spear was sinking back inside the other end as the handle spun.

"A timber-jack!" As Jessie said it, we shouted and ran. With our axes, we sniped the ends of the logs round, so they'd run easier through the bush. We propped timber-jacks against the sides of the logs and rolled them. We jacked the ends so they slid. We worked them down into the creek.

We felled tall narrow-trunked trees we called rickers, and made chutes down the hill. We worked the kauri logs to the top, jacked them into the chute, and they slid down so fast the timber smoked. We jacked the logs along rolling roads. We skidded them behind bullocks, their sniped ends riding over boulders and fallen trees. We pit-sawed wooden rails and made tramways, and pulled the logs on bogies behind horses, and rolled them down the tip head into the creek. As far as we could walk and see, the bottom and sides of the creek were lined with kauri logs.

"Now you know what a scarf is," said Aunt Effie, her voice fading away. "And a back-cut, and a timber-jack ..." The green light in which we had lived for so long was turning dark. Somewhere a fire burned, and the light fell across Aunt Effie's face as she closed her eyes and snored.

We stared at her and at each other. We were lying

amongst the dogs and eiderdowns on the foot of Aunt Effie's enormous bed. Quietly, so we didn't wake her, we were sliding to the floor when a gruff voice whispered, "Watch out for the Bugaboo!" and we ran screaming downstairs.

Note: "Scarf, back-cut, snipe, rolling road, ricker, bogie, timber-jack! I try to tell Aunt Effie it's not right, using such difficult words in front of the little ones. But nobody ever takes any notice of old me." —Daisy.

Chapter Four

How the Treaty was Signed

"*Daisy-Mabel*-Johnny-Flossie-Lynda-Stan-Howard-Marge-Stuart! Marie-Peter-Colleen-Alwyn-Bryce-Jack! Ann-Jazz-Becky-Jane-Isaac-David-Victor! Casey-Lizzie-Jared-Jess!" We ran and climbed on Aunt Effie's bed amongst dogs, timber-jacks, sawdust, and hard little green pine cones.

"I was telling you how Captain Flash and I danced on the stump of the giant kauri while Herodotus played the musical saw," said Aunt Effie. "We sawed off the butt log, Herodotus dug a pit, and I jacked the log across. You've all used a timber-jack, so you know what they look like," Aunt Effie said and stared at Jessie and Lizzie.

"Captain Flash stood on top of the log, Herodotus got down in the pit, and they tried sawing the log into planks along the lines I'd chalked. But the saw wouldn't cut!"

"Why not?"

"It was a twelve-foot, drag-tooth, cross-cut saw," said Auntie Effie. She stared fiercely at Lizzie and Jessie again. "You've used one so you know it's for cutting across the grain of the tree. But, when you're cutting the log into planks, you're sawing with the grain. So you need a different kind, a rip-saw.

"I set up the blacksmith's forge and made a pit-saw. Captain Flash climbed on top of the log again and pulled the saw up. Herodotus climbed into the pit and pulled the saw down. Up and down, up and down they sawed, Captain Flash complaining all the time."

"Why did he complain?"

"That log was so thick, he got dizzy if he looked down. I turned his ear-trumpet round so he couldn't see through the eyeholes. Then he said Herodotus wasn't doing his share. Then he said it was dank and cold inside his ear-trumpet. It was, too. That log was so thick through, his head was in the clouds.

"Then Herodotus complained Captain Flash's sweat kept dropping on him. He said Captain Flash kept spitting on his head. And doing worse things, too."

"What worse things?"

"Think!" Aunt Effie told Lizzie. "In the end, I made them swap places. When Captain Flash complained about sawdust trickling down his neck, I made a tin collar and fastened it around his shoulders, under his ear-trumpet.

"From end to end they sawed that huge butt log in half. Then they sawed one half into half again. I jacked one huge flitch back over the pit and chalked the cuts. They sawed, the planks fell away, and I stacked and filleted them to dry. We built a shipyard, sheds, a house, a wharf. Still the Captain and Herodotus sawed planks off that flitch: one quarter of the butt log of the huge kauri.

"As the timber seasoned, I built a thirty-two gun frigate. I laid the keel, fastened the stern-post and the stem to it, put up the frames, planked the hull, and laid the decks. While the Captain and Herodotus sawed, I felled some rickers and adzed them for masts and spars.

"I cast the anchors and cables. I cast thirty-two cannons and the twelve-pound cannon-balls for them. I cast four brass nine-pound chasers and their cannon-balls. I forged and hammered and cast the bolts and nuts and the hawse-pipe. The keel bolts, the pintles and gudgeons, and the steering chains. I made the brass work for a telescope, melted sand to make glass, and ground the lenses. I wove sails from flax. I twisted and laid up the ropes for the rigging. There's many a mile of running and standing rigging on a thirty-two gun frigate."

"Where did you get the iron to cast all those cannons and anchors and bolts?" asked Lizzie.

"In those days, there were abandoned Japanese cars lying about all over Waharoa. I mixed them with black iron-sand off the beach and melted them down in my biggest camp oven."

"Oh!" said Lizzie.

"All this time, Captain Flash and Herodotus sawed on. At last, I told them: 'The ship's finished. You can knock off now.'

"Back in England, it had taken a thousand oaks to build the ship Captain Flash sank," said Aunt Effie. "Here in Waharoa, we'd built the dam, the booms, the scow, the shipyards, sheds, a house, a wharf, and a three-masted frigate, and there was enough timber left over to build most of Auckland and Wellington when we founded them a hundred years later, and we'd still only sawn up one flitch, one quarter of the butt log of that giant kauri."

"Oh?" said Lizzie.

"I tell you what," said Aunt Effie. "Kauris were kauris in those days!"

"Oh?"

"Well," said Aunt Effie, staring at Lizzie, "you've cut down a kauri, so you know how big they are.

"We launched our ship. Captain Flash named it the *Dainty Ankle* in memory of the first time we danced in the moonlight, crossing the Indian Ocean. He could be so romantic," Aunt Effie sighed, "so long as you didn't look at his head stuck in the ear-trumpet.

"We were admiring our frigate when a Maori chief appeared doing a haka. He didn't have on a stitch of clothes, so Captain Flash clapped his hands over my eyes. Luckily, I could see between his fingers. Oh!" she sighed again, "the chief was a fine figure of a man. Much better looking than the Captain. We shook hands and rubbed noses."

"It's called a hongi," said Daisy, who thought she knew everything.

"My, what a fund of information we are today!" Aunt Effie shifted her feet under the eiderdown. Daisy was shoved against Kaiser who bit her. Aunt Effie handed her a bottle. "Old Puckeroo Rubbing Alcohol for Athletes," she said as Daisy snivelled and rubbed it on the tooth marks. Aunt Effie tipped the bottle up and emptied what was left down her throat.

"I thought you said it was rubbing alcohol?" Daisy whimpered.

"Watch out Kaiser doesn't bite you again." Aunt Effie rubbed her throat vigorously.

"The Maori chief whose name was Rangi expressed himself in the most elegant English," she went on. "He said we'd cut down his kauri without permission. He was very sorry, but he would have to kill and eat us and send our buttons back to Queen Victorious.

"'Disgraceful!' Captain Flash told him. 'Cannibalism is so uncivilised!' I felt my buttons," said Aunt Effie, "and thought of the cabin boy, the cook, and the carpenter.

"'Chief Rangi, I have a message to you from Queen Victorious.' Captain Flash undid his shiny buttons and pulled out a roll of paper. 'Queen Victorious offers you a fair price for your kauris, your land, and your racehorses. In return, you and your fortunate people can become her subjects. Sign here, please!'"

"'What is the message called?' asked Rangi.

"'The Treaty of Waharoa,' said Captain Flash. 'I will read it to you.' He cleared his throat, looked through the eyeholes of the brass ear-trumpet, and shouted the first line of the Treaty aloud. 'KO WIKITORIOUS, TE KUINI O INGARINGI!'

"'Why is he bellowing?' Rangi asked me.

"'Because he thinks you can understand English only if he shouts it very loud and very slow,' I told him.

"'But that's not English he's shouting. That's Maori!'

"'Perhaps,' I said, 'Captain Flash is shouting it very loud and very slow because he can't understand it himself.'

"Rangi laughed. 'Here,' he said to Captain Flash, 'give us your Treaty.' He took out the first ballpoint we had seen and, using his right hand then his left, then his right again, he signed the Treaty several times. 'I might as well sign for the other chiefs while I'm about it.'

"Captain Flash rolled up the Treaty of Waharoa, sewed it inside a piece of green canvas to keep it safe, and painted it with tar to keep it waterproof. 'I'll take it to Queen Victorious at once!'

"Back on the *Dainty Ankle*, Herodotus swung the gig aboard and ran up and down the masts, bending on the sails. He played the fiddle and and sang and stamped and tramped around the capstan, broke out the anchor, and got the cable straight up and down. Captain Flash fired a salute to Rangi. As the smoke rolled across the water and the twenty-one guns boomed, the sails filled. Herodotus catted the anchor, and the *Dainty Ankle* swept down the harbour on the outgoing tide.

"As they passed the kauri stump on which Rangi and I stood waving, Captain Flash bent over, and Herodotus clapped a gun-tackle on the end of the ear -trumpet. He pulled at the rope, and it came off with a loud suck! Captain Flash danced with delight on the deck of the *Dainty Ankle*. I didn't like to call out that his head had been squashed inside so long, it now grew to a sharp point. He put the ear-trumpet to his mouth and shouted through it.

"'Queen Victorious will reward me for getting you to sign the Treaty of Waharoa. I'll never have to go to sea again. Ha! Ha! Ha!'

"As they sailed over the bar that was very rough, I could see Captain Flash's pointed head being sick over the side. Herodotus had taken the wheel."

"But they left you behind," said Lizzie. "I thought Captain Flash loved you? And you said Herodotus was your friend!"

"To tell the truth," said Aunt Effie, "I was somewhat relieved to see the back of them both. Captain Flash was not nearly as good-looking as Rangi, and Herodotus had begun to give me the creeps. Would you feel comfortable with a huge grey rat who insisted on sleeping under your bed?"

We thought of the Bugaboo and shook our heads.

"What did the Treaty of Waharoa say?" asked Casey.

"It said that Rangi gave away everything he owned to Queen Victorious. In return, he could go on living in Waharoa."

"But he could do that already. Without giving anything away!" Jessie cried.

"I said that to Rangi," Aunt Effie nodded, "but he just smiled. 'When you signed the Treaty, you signed away your lands, your rivers, and your kauri trees!' I told him.

"'Not when they read the Treaty properly,' said Rangi.

He was a remarkably good-looking man when he smiled. My heart beat faster. He laughed, and his teeth flashed white against his brown skin. I do like a man who enjoys a good laugh. And one who can make me laugh."

"Why did he laugh?" Lizzie asked. "He'd just signed everything away to Queen Victorious!"

Aunt Effie smiled and snapped her teeth. "Rangi said to me, 'Wait till Queen Victorious sees how I signed the Treaty.' He laughed, and I stared at him. 'Yes,' he said, 'I signed it: Mickey Mouse, Pluto, and Donald Duck!'"

Note: *"Pit-saws, rip-saws, flitches, chasers, hawse-pipes, catting the anchor, capstan! And just who are Mickey Mouse, Pluto, and Donald Duck? More disreputable friends of Aunt Effie, I'll be bound!"* —Daisy.

Chapter Five

Building a Kauri Dam

"*I'd had to clap* my own hands over my eyes after Captain Flash had gone, but now I was able to take them away and admire Rangi openly," said Aunt Effie. "To sign the Treaty of Waharoa, he wore an admiral's uniform Queen Victorious had sent. His tattooed face, what he called his moko, went well with it. Besides being well-built and well-dressed, he was also well-spoken, well-educated, and well-mannered.

"He told stories of sailing on whalers and sealers. He described crossing the Tasman with cargoes of corrugated iron, pine logs, and potatoes for the Sydney market. He showed me his schooners loading abacuses, ukeleles, and greenstone tikis for San Francisco.

"'Why sell to the Yanks?' I asked Rangi.

"'The Poms are a nation of mere shopkeepers,' he told me. 'The American dollar's worth more than their pound.' He took off his plumed hat, swept it across his heart, dropped on one knee and oh, most elegantly, he kissed my hand!

"'Will you marry me?' he asked.

"What could I say?" Aunt Effie fluttered her curly eyelashes and looked around us. "He was a fine-looking man who could make me laugh, and he looked so dashing with his moko and his admiral's uniform jingling with medals and brass buttons. I wasn't sorry to have seen the last of Captain Flash. Even though he was a very good dancer, the moment I saw the pointed shape his head had taken inside the ear-trumpet, I knew I couldn't marry him."

"Did you marry Rangi?" asked Lizzie.

"I promised I would." Aunt Effie looked down and blushed. "We fixed the day. All we needed was a missionary to perform the ceremony. Unfortunately, the only one available was at Kororareka in the Bay of Islands. Rangi sailed there and brought him back, but the missionary was so drunk he couldn't remember the words of the wedding service. We tried several times but couldn't catch him sober. In the end, Rangi had to leave me weeping on the end of the wharf and sail for San Francisco with a load of pine needles, huia feathers, and posters encouraging tourists to come to Waharoa."

"What was the name of the drunken missionary?"

"Samuel something or other. He was a bad-tempered devil, too, when he woke up sober and found Rangi had sailed for San Francisco without him."

"What happened when Queen Victorious found Mickey Mouse, Pluto, and Donald Duck had signed the Treaty of Waharoa?" asked Lizzie.

"She ordered Captain Flash hanged in chains at

Execution Dock. With a cutlass, Herodotus prodded him up the mast and out along the yard-arm of the *Dainty Ankle*. Queen Victorious beat on a big drum. Herodotus dropped the noose over the dear Captain's head. Queen Victorious beat the drum louder. Captain Flash danced a last hornpipe, and Herodotus pushed him off the yard-arm."

Lizzie stuck her fingers in her ears. Jessie covered her eyes. Aunt Effie took a bottle of Old Puckeroo Foot Balm from under her pillow, swallowed a good gulp, and said, "Not only was his head very pointed, but Captain Flash had no neck. The noose tightened but just slipped off. Instead of hanging, he fell from the yard-arm, swam underwater and climbed up the other side of the *Dainty Ankle* as Herodotus unfurled the sails and cast off. Queen Victorious fired a cannon but missed. She dived into the dock and swam after them, but her heavy crown slowed her down, and they got away."

Aunt Effie finished the bottle of foot balm, flung it under her bed, and closed her eyes. We were just sliding to the floor, when a rough voice said, "Watch out for the Bugaboo!" and we screamed and ran, leaving the little ones behind. They caught up, crying and pinching us for running away, and we all fled downstairs.

Next time we heard Aunt Effie calling our names, we hardly had time to climb on her enormous bed before she went on with her story.

"Meanwhile, I was still standing on the end of the wharf in Waharoa, crying my heart out for Rangi, when I heard Captain Flash's voice raised in a throbbing love song. He came sailing up the harbour with Herodotus at the wheel of the *Dainty Ankle*. Captain Flash was wearing his best uniform. He looked very elegant as far as the shoulders, but from there up everything went into a point. He put a brass speaking-trumpet to his mouth.

"'Effie, ahoy!' he yelled. It was very loud and embarrassing."

"Why were you embarrassed?" asked Casey.

"I could tell by the throb in his voice that Captain Flash was still in love with me. And just at that moment, Rangi sailed in from San Francisco with a preacher to marry us. Unfortunately, while they'd both been away, the drunken missionary, Samuel, had also fallen in love with me. So I had three eminently suitable men, each wanting to marry me. What was I to do?"

We stared at Aunt Effie and shook our heads. The dogs woke and grumbled.

"I hope you did the right thing!" said Daisy in her most proper voice.

"Down Caligula! Down Brutus!" Aunt Effie ordered. "Let go of Daisy!" she told Boris.

"I married the lot of them!" she said. "Oh, not all at once. Samuel had no staying power and died young. Well, he had a liver the size of a pumpkin from all that drinking. And Captain Flash didn't last long. Besides, all the Maori kids called him Pointy because of the shape of his head. They fell around laughing every time they saw him. For the rest of his life the poor man couldn't get a hat that fitted him. And, after he died of disappointment, I married Rangi."

"Did you have any children?"

"I had children by all my marriages, those three and all the others," said Aunt Effie.

"Did you get married more than three times?" Lizzie asked.

"Men were no more reliable then than they are today. They were always getting squashed under trees or drowned in rivers: there were no bridges in Waharoa then. Quite a few fell over the edge, sailing around the world to Sydney, and were never seen again. I don't know how many husbands I lost in those early years."

"How many children did you have?" asked Jessie.

"I lost count," said Aunt Effie. "All those names! And it all happened so long ago. I'm not just your aunt, you know. I might be your great-aunt. And your great-great-aunt. And to the younger ones, I'm your great-great-great-aunt. To some of you I'm probably your great-great-great-grandmother. For all I know, some of you might be my great-great-great-great-grandchildren."

We wanted to know more about her husbands and children, but Aunt Effie pulled a pipe from under her pillow. "Today I thought I might show you how to build a dam and drive the kauri logs."

"Oh, yes!" we cried – all of us but Daisy who was looking at Aunt Effie's pipe. Peter tried to shut her up, but it was too late.

"You're not supposed to smoke while we're here," Daisy told Aunt Effie. "It's not good for children to have to become passive smokers. Eek!" she squealed as Nero bit her.

"Proper little Miss Righteous, aren't we!" said Aunt

Effie. She blew, and a bubble rose from her pipe and turned red, orange, yellow, green, blue, indigo, and violet. It shivered and grew bigger until it covered Aunt Effie, the dogs, all of us, and her enormous bed. It grew still bigger until it covered the furniture, the suit of armour, the crystal chandelier with a thousand candles that Aunt Effie used for a reading lamp, and the velvet curtains that hung over the windows, rich with dust and specks of sunlight. The colours stretched and wobbled on the bubble until it burst. Bang!

We were standing by the same creek where we had left all the kauri logs lying in the bed and on the banks. We were all wearing boots, moleskin trousers and blue Crimean shirts.

"Daisy-Mabel-Johnny-Flossie-Lynda-Stan-Howard-Marge-Stuart!" Aunt Effie called. She gave them picks and shovels and set them to building a coffer-dam to turn the water through a channel they dug down one side, so the creek bed was left dry.

"Marie-Peter-Colleen-Alwyn-Bryce-Jack!" Aunt Effie set us digging out all the dirt and mud in the dry creek bed till we got down to solid rock. As we got hot, we threw off the shirts and worked in our flannel singlets.

"Ann-Jazz-Becky-Jane-Isaac-David-Victor!" They were set to cutting down kauri rickers – tall straight, young trees – and squaring their sides with broad-axes.

"Casey-Lizzie-Jared-Jess!" They cut poles and put up the framework of a hut. They thatched the walls and both sides of the roof with nikau leaves. They built a huge chimney one end, a table down the middle, and bunks around the walls.

We chopped a trench in the rock right across the dry creek-bed. Into it we dropped a squared log so it fitted snug. That log Aunt Effie called the sill. About thirty feet above the creek, we dragged a long log across and anchored it into holes we chopped into the rock walls. Aunt Effie smacked the log with her hand. "The main stringer!" she said.

"When the dam's full," she said, "the stringer takes most of the strain. We'll have to tom it up against all that pressure."

"Sill?" said Daisy. "Stringer? Tom? I don't understand."

Aunt Effie stared at Daisy. "Use your ears and eyes!" she said. "You'll learn fast enough."

Daisy's mouth turned down. Aunt Effie grinned. "It's like reading a book," she told her. "If you stop to look up every word you don't understand, you'll never finish the story. Just keep going, and you'll pick up what they mean. And you can stop pulling that face, Daisy. The wind might change, and you'll be stuck with it for the rest of your life!"

The rest of us laughed, but Daisy looked even more dismal. "Sill! Stringer! Tom!" she muttered.

"I'll tell you what," said Aunt Effie. "You make a list of all the words you don't understand, and we'll explain them at the back of this book. And we'll call it Daisy's Glossary."

"Are we writing a book?" asked Daisy, and we all stared at Aunt Effie.

"Of course!" She stared straight back at us. "What do you think we're doing here? Now, let's get on with it. And, remember, if you don't understand a word, have a look in Daisy's Glossary. Any other silly questions?"

Without waiting for an answer, Aunt Effie bounded on top of the main stringer. Her axe over her left shoulder taking the weight of the timber-jack over her right shoulder, she strode along whistling "God Defend Queen Victorious"

"You'd think she'd slip!" said Bryce.

"Not Aunt Effie!" Marie told him.

"Heave up those rafters," Aunt Effie yelled. The rafters were squared baulks of heavy timber. We fitted their bottom ends into holes cut into the creek-bed above the sill. Aunt Effie spiked and bolted their top ends against the stringer. We watched, but she didn't slip. Instead, she sat on one of the rafters, gave a whoop, and slid down beside us.

"You want to make sure you're not sliding against the grain," she said to Daisy. "Or you could get your bum full of splinters!"

Daisy turned away with a disapproving look and added a word to her list.

We jacked a smaller stringer across to take the weight of the gate. We leaned and bolted more rafters into place. "I know what a stringer is," said Jared.

"And a sill," said Jessie.

"And a rafter," said Casey.

"I know what a splinter is," said Lizzie who'd slid down a rafter. "I got one in my bum!"

We got sawdust in our hair and down our necks as we pit-sawed planks to finish the face of the dam. We hit our thumbs, driving spikes with heavy hammers. We cut our fingers and arms and legs, but Aunt Effie stitched us up with a curved sacking needle and long hairs she pulled out of her own head, and we worked on.

We were so busy building the dam, we forgot we had ever done anything else. And in the middle of all our work, there came a bellow like the bray of a giant donkey.

Note: "Crimean shirt, coffer-dam, nikau, sill, main stringer, tom, baulk, rafter. Why do I have to do all the work? So other people can just look up the glossary at the back of the book. Why can't they listen and work out for themselves what the words mean? As I have to." —Daisy.

Chapter Six

Tripping the Dam

The terrifying bray was Aunt Effie blowing on a cow's horn. "Daisy-Mabel-Johnny-Flossie-Lynda-Stan-Howard-Marge-Stuart! Marie-Peter-Colleen-Alwyn-Bryce-Jack! Ann-Jazz-Becky-Jane-Isaac-David-Victor! Casey-Lizzie-Jared-Jess! Knock off for lunch!"

We sat each side of the long table down the middle of the nikau whare, and Aunt Effie heaped our plates with pigeon, moa, and kiwi stew out of an iron camp oven. We were so hungry, we forgot we didn't like stew. With a crosscut Aunt Effie sawed up a round loaf of bread she tipped out of another camp oven and rolled over to the table. We sniffed the smell of fresh-baked bread, slapped on butter while it was still hot, and washed down the feathers and beaks in our stew with mugs of sweet strong tea.

In the afternoon, we built the gate on our dam, planks dangling on lengths of wire. They were held in place by a big tom with a trigger pulled by a wire rope. We chopped holes in the rock of the creek-bed and tommed up the rafters with more rickers to help the main stringer hold back all that weight of water.

"Daisy-Mabel-Johnny-Flossie-Lynda-Stan-Howard-Marge-Stuart! Knock down your coffer-dam!"

The creek ran down its bed again and pooled against the sill. Water squirted between the bottom planks.

"Marie-Peter-Colleen-Alwyn-Bryce-Jack! Ann-Jazz-Becky-Jane-Isaac-David-Victor! Casey-Lizzie-Jared-Jess! Fill these sacks with bookau."

"I think the proper name for it is pukahu," said Daisy. Unfortunately hers was a carrying voice.

Aunt Effie pushed over a nikau so it flattened Daisy as it fell. "Poor child!" Aunt Effie said. She stood Daisy up, brushed her down, and whacked out a chunk of nikau heart for her to chew on.

"It tastes lovely!" said Daisy. "Rich and creamy."

"I think the Maori name for it is rito, korito if you want to be exact," said Aunt Effie. "Me, I call it 'millionaire's salad'."

"Why do you call it that?" asked Lizzie.

"Because you have to kill the tree to get a feed of it. Now," Aunt Effie looked around, "where's all that bookau?"

Around the bottom of the big kauri trees, leaves, flakes of bark, and knobs of kauri gum had fallen for a couple of thousand years. Covered with ferns, it was heaped twice as high as us, the stuff Aunt Effie called bookau. We filled our sacks, carried them down, and covered the cracks between the planks. As the water rose, its pressure carried and worked the bookau into the cracks where it swelled and stopped the leaks. The pool deepened against the dam and backed up, a long narrow lake. One by one, the logs in the creek bed stirred, rolled, and floated.

There were still a few logs at the top of the chute. We jacked and sent them whistling and smoking down – Smash! – into the water! Waves set the other logs jobbling against each other.

Lizzie climbed on the last log, to ride it down the chute. "You'll get squashed flat as a pikelet if the log rolls," Aunt Effie told her. "So thin and flat, we could spit through you!"

Lizzie cried at that but cheered up when Aunt Effie gave her what she called a pike-pole. We all cut long poles and ran out on the logs, balancing as they turned under our feet, and lined them up before the gate. A few leaks squirted, but the dam held. "I wouldn't like to be standing below," said Casey, "if it gave way!"

"Time for smoko! We need a lot more water for a really good drive."

Rain began as we followed Aunt Effie into the whare. The green gutters of the nikau leaves caught every drop and carried it away. Thunder clouted and clumped up and down the valley. Lightning zigzagged so close we could smell it burn the air. After a billy of tea and date scones made in the camp oven, we punched in the corners of our sacks, pulled them over our heads, and climbed up the hill.

We spun the long S-shaped handles on the timber

jacks. The logs turned and rolled and sloshed through the mud. Downhill they slid faster and faster over the wet ground. The ones that bogged down, we jacked on to rolling roads and tumbled them to the water. By dark, the dam was nearly full to the top. Several logs sank. "Sinkers," Aunt Effie said, "full of gum, but they'll get swept through with the rest – with any luck."

We had eel and morepork stew for our tea, and dried our sacks and clothes on lines across the great fireplace. We scrubbed out the camp ovens with handfuls of sand. The little ones were so tired they fell asleep and tumbled headfirst into theirs. They had to be lifted out, pegged on the lines across the fireplace, and dried before they could go to bed.

"Casey-Elizabeth-Jared-Jessica!" Aunt Effie unpegged and tossed them up on their bunks. They rolled into their blankets and were asleep at once. "Ann-Jazz-Becky-Jane-Isaac-David-Victor!" Aunt Effie threw them up into the next row of bunks. "Marie-Peter-Colleen-Alwyn-Bryce-Jack!" She piggybacked us across the hut and tipped us over her head into our bunks. "Daisy-Mabel-Johnny-Flossie-Lynda-Stan-Howard-Marge-Stuart!" She gave them a leg-up into their bunks. And then we must have slept. With not a thought of the Bugaboo.

We woke in our own beds at home. "I want to see the dam tripped," Lizzie sobbed. "I want to see the timber drive."

"Daisy-Mabel-Johnny-Flossie-Lynda-Stan-Howard-Marge-Stuart! Marie-Peter-Colleen-Alwyn-Bryce-Jack!

Ann-Jazz-Becky-Jane-Isaac-David-Victor! Casey-Lizzie-Jared-Jess!"

"It's Aunt Effie!" we gasped. "Quick!"

Still in our pyjamas we ran up the stairs. "Coming, Aunt Effie!" We climbed up on her enormous bed, shoving the bad-tempered dogs aside, making nests for ourselves amongst the eiderdowns.

"Who's snivelling?" asked Aunt Effie.

"Lizzie wants to see the dam tripped!" we all said together.

"We built it," said Aunt Effie. "Isn't that enough?"

"I want to see it tripped," Lizzie grizzled.

"We all want to see it tripped! We want to see a timber drive!"

"No need to shout." Aunt Effie scrabbled around under the pillow and found her pipe. She felt under her pillow again and brought out a black bottle labelled "Old Puckeroo Extra Strong Scotch Embrocation. Good for Both Horses and Men."

"You're not going to start drinking at this time of the morning!" said our cousin Daisy in her shocked voice.

"Just a drop of tonic to cleanse the blood. What a shame Brutus bit you, dear." There was a wail from Daisy. Aunt Effie rubbed a bit of Old Puckeroo on Daisy's foot and took a swig herself. "That's better!" She gargled with a noise like somebody pulling the chain.

Aunt Effie shook her head. "Ahhh!" she said. "Ahhh–Choo!" Her giant sneeze blew us all off the end of her enormous bed. We landed outside our nikau whare and looked down at a huge lake. The rain during the night had filled the dam to the top. More and more logs had come down. We ran across them to the far side and back again, and never saw the water between them.

"Let's trip the dam," said Aunt Effie.

"Breakfast first," said Daisy. "It's important to start the day with a good meal!"

Attila snarled and bit Brutus. Their thick tails swung together and clouted Daisy into the water. Aunt Effie dipped her out on the end of a pike-pole.

"Dry yourself by the fire and start making the porridge. The rest of us will trip the dam. We can always have breakfast afterwards. Here, everyone, grab hold of this."

We took hold of the wire tripping-rope.

"Whatever you do, don't fall in. You'll be squashed into mud sandwiches. Ready? Steady! Pull!"

We pulled together. The tripping-rope swung a block of heavy rata that knocked out the trip-hook. The tripping-pole – the big tom that held the gate closed – fell away. The gate-planks swung open on their wires, and the lake lurched forward. The rumble of logs, the gush of water! We couldn't hear Daisy even though she ran out of the nikau whare and stood screaming in her loud voice right beside us.

As if they were corks, the huge logs rode through the gate and boomed down the flooded creek. One great log, squashed between two others, shot in the air like an orange-pip. It cleared the top of the dam and bounced thirteen times off the logs below.

The mountains groaned and swayed. We fell over,

climbed to our feet, and fell over again as the valley trembled. David and Victor said they could hear the trees on the ridges scraping backwards and forwards against the sky. It went on for about an hour until the dam was empty, water and logs gone in the wild rush downstream.

We closed the gate, put the tom back in place, the trip-hook, and the tripping-rope. "A pretty clean sweep," said Aunt Effie, "but we'll fill the dam just in case."

She gave a mournful bray on the cow horn. "All right, Daisy," she said. "We'll have our breakfast now." Before we could sit down inside the whare, there was a rushing wind like the great sneeze Aunt Effie gave that morning, and we were flying through the air. A sudden bump, and we were sitting on the foot of Aunt Effie's enormous bed.

She was snuggling down in her green canvas invalid's pyjamas. Her eyes closed, and she began to snore. Lizzie jumped halfway to the door, hit the floor running, and the rest of us followed. If the Bugaboo was waiting to catch us, he was out of luck.

Note: "*Nikau, whare, bookau, rito, pike-pole, sinker, tripping-rope, tripping-pole? How many more?*" —Daisy.

55

Chapter Seven

What a Muddle!

We were replacing a strainer-post the bulls had pushed over in the north corner of their paddock. Alwyn groaned and bellowed, stamping his feet.

"Stop teasing the bulls," Peter said. "Look what they did to the old strainer!"

Alwyn pulled faces at the bulls instead until they chased him up the acorn tree in the middle of their paddock. He sat on a branch, poking out his tongue and chucking acorns at them until they trundled like trains to dig their horns into the tree, trying to shake him down.

Marie hammered in a couple of totara staples, twisted the wire back on itself and tucked the end under so nobody could sprag themselves. We put the wire-strainer and the tools into a sugarbag, threw it on the konaki, and hung on to each other shrieking while Major pulled us back to the barn.

We'd unharnessed Major, lifted off his heavy collar, and were watching him have a roll when we heard,

"Daisy-Mabel-Johnny-Flossie-Lynda-Stan-Howard-Marge-Stuart-Peter-Marie-Colleen-Alwyn-Bryce-Jack-Ann-Jazz-Beck-Jane-Isaac-David-Victor-Casey-Lizzie-Jared-Jess!"

"Who's missing?" said Aunt Effie as we settled on her bed. "Daisy-Mabel-Johnny-Flossie-Lynda-Stan-Howard-Marge-Stuart? Peter-Marie-Colleen-Alwyn-Bryce-Jack? Ann-Jazz-Beck-Jane-Isaac-David-Victor-Casey-Lizzie-Jared or Jess?"

"The bulls have got Alwyn up the acorn tree," we said.

Aunt Effie nodded. There was a bellow, a flash of bulls' horns and Alwyn flew in the window, and landed beside us on the foot of Aunt Effie's enormous bed. At once, he barked at the dogs who lifted their heads and growled back. Aunt Effie grinned to herself.

We knew Daisy had been dying to ask her a question. Before we could stop her, she said, "Aunt Effie, if you can't remember how many husbands you had, how do you know which of us is which?"

"Does it matter?" asked Aunt Effie.

"It does to me!"

Aunt Effie nodded. "It all happened so long ago, no-one can be sure. Some of you are called this, and some of you are called that. Don't tease the dogs, Peter-Marie-Colleen-Alwyn-Bryce-Jack." She turned to Lizzie and said, "What's your second name?"

"Ann," said Lizzie.

"That's what I mean!" said Aunt Effie. "Ann might be your aunty."

"But you said she's my cousin."

"She might be your cousin, too. But I think her second name is Rangi, so, if she's your aunt, you could be related to the Maori chief who signed the Treaty of Waharoa."

"But he signed himself Mickey Mouse, Pluto, and Donald Duck."

"He had lots of other names, too," said Aunt Effie. "When Rangi and I were married, he signed the register Tom Thumb. The American preacher who married us asked him about that.

"'That's my other name,' Rangi told him. 'Tame Iti. Tame means Tommy, and Iti's Little. So Tom Little, or Little Tom. So sometimes I sign myself Tom Thumb.'

"'I suppose it's all right,' the American preacher said.

"'What's in a name?' asked Rangi. And since there didn't seem to be a sensible answer to that question, the preacher shut up."

Aunt Effie smiled around us. "I am dying, Egypt, dying!" She gave a gigantic sneeze. But we hung on to the eiderdown and didn't fly off the foot of her enormous bed this time.

"Where did all the kauri logs go, Aunt Effie?" asked Jessie. "After we tripped the dam?"

Aunt Effie felt for a hanky and blew her nose so loud our ears flapped, the dogs barked at Alwyn, and we fell off her enormous bed. When we stood up, we were following the log drive down the creek.

We ran and climbed and slipped and fell, pushing logs with our long pike-poles. Just when the logs began to slow, and the last of the water trickled away beneath them, Aunt Effie disappeared. We climbed down into the dry creek bed and were looking at one log, all split and tasselled where it had bumped and frayed against rocks, when there came a great thundering noise.

"Get out!" shouted Peter and Marie.

The rest of us scrambled up the bank, but Daisy stood in the creek-bed and said to Marie, "You can't tell me what to do!"

"Quick!" Marie screamed.

"You're not my boss!"

"Don't argue, Daisy!" we cried.

"I'm older than you," she told Marie. "And you!" she told Peter.

"She's tripped the dam again!" Peter shouted, but Daisy couldn't hear him because she was shouting something back.

Froth, bits of gum, leaves, and branches flying back off its winged billow, a giant wave thundered down the valley above Daisy. Lightning flashed and forked along its crest. Across the front of the flood came Aunt Effie, standing and yahooing on a pit-sawn plank like a surf-board. She flung Daisy on to the bank as the fresh drive picked up the stranded logs and swept them away.

"Huh!" said Daisy, but her voice trembled, and we noticed her fingers crossed behind her back.

We caught up to Aunt Effie near the booms at the top of the tidal waters: long logs fastened together across the mangrove-lined river. We hammered in iron dogs, bored holes with augers, and chained our logs together in a great raft with a nikau whare on top. When the tide turned, we opened the boom, shoved with our pike-poles, and the raft carried out on the glistening river.

We spent our days pushing each other in, diving, swimming, fishing, and sleeping in the shade of the nikau whare. Aunt Effie said it would take about two years to drift down to the mouth of the Mangrove River.

"I think I'd better teach you some lessons," she said, "or you'll get behind all the other kids at school."

Lizzie said, "No!" Jessie said, "Won't!" Jared said, "You can't make me!" Casey said, "Nor me!" The rest of us tried crying, but Aunt Effie taught us our arithmetic and spelling and reading and writing. We sang, "One and one are two. Two and two are four." Our sad voices echoed between the mangroves as we drifted, anchoring when the tide turned and came in, and pulling up the anchors and drifting towards the mouth again when the tide turned and ran out.

One afternoon, Daisy said, "I love our arithmetic lessons." Next morning Aunt Effie said she couldn't be bothered, and we spent the rest of the two years shoving each other off the raft, diving, swimming, fishing, and sleeping in the shade of the nikau whare. When we thought we couldn't remember having ever lived any other way, we came in sight of the sea, paddled the raft into Back Bay, and chained a boom across the mouth.

"We're there," said Aunt Effie, and her voice sounded sad.

Next morning we stood in single file on the big butt log and poled it across the river and up Mother Browne's Creek. There, Mr Browne had built a small dam. The water from it ran down a long-legged trestle, poured out the end, and turned a water-wheel. The water-wheel turned a shaft. The shaft turned a huge breaking-down saw that cut our log into flitches.

We helped Mr Browne saw the flitches into planks. "It's faster than pit-sawing," said Jared.

"You wait," said Mr Browne. "I'm getting a steam engine to run the mill. It'll be twice as fast."

"Wow!"

"It'll also be ten times noisier, twenty times dirtier, and fifty times more dangerous!" Mother Browne complained.

"Now, Mother," said Mr Browne. "That's progress!"

We stacked the planks on the beach at the mouth of the Mangrove River. While the timber seasoned, Aunt Effie told us about the times when she was a young woman at the Bay.

"Rangi, or Tom Thumb, or Tame Iti as he sometimes called himself, disappeared at sea," she said. "He was sailing a cargo of skateboards and electric guitars to San Francisco."

"Did they make electric guitars in New Zealand?" asked Daisy in her knowing voice.

"They did then!" said Aunt Effie. "Or maybe they were acoustic guitars. Who cares? Anyway, there I was left with five children from my marriage to Captain Flash; four from my marriage to Samuel, the missionary; and three from my marriage to Rangi. The older children were a great help with the little ones.

"It must have been about that time I met the boat-builder, Mr Singh."

"He sounds like an Indian!" said Daisy.

"Such a beautiful man!" said Aunt Effie. "With eyes so dark they made me go all gooey and knock-kneed. We were married before a Justice of the Peace, and Ranjit Singh began a boat-building yard."

"My second name's Singh," said Peter.

"And mine's Ranjit," said Jared.

"Well, you could be the great-great-great-great-grand-children of Ranjit Singh," said Aunt Effie. "But I wouldn't bet on it."

"Why not?" Jared wanted to know.

"It's all so long ago," said Aunt Effie, "and I was never the best at remembering names. Besides, we were married only long enough to have two more children, when Ranjit got squashed. I'd warned him again and again not to stand on the slipway taking photos as his

63

schooners were launched."

"Did they have cameras when you were a girl?" asked Isaac.

"They were around. I'm sure there's photos some-where of my wedding at Kororareka to Rangi, your great-great-great-great-grandfather."

Aunt Effie thought for a moment and heaved a sigh. "My wedding dress!" she exclaimed. "It was made of lace-bark boiled and bleached so fine, it made me cry just to look at it. Underneath I wore ten petticoats stiff-ened with the finest whalebone. My veil was of rare white maidenhair fern from the Vast Untrodden Ureweras, and my train was gold brocade fifty yards long. You all stood in two rows behind me and carried it."

"But we weren't born then!" we said.

"You've forgotten, that's all! Think hard, and you'll remember."

"Anyway," she heaved another sigh, "I soon remarried the Harbour Master and we had three babies, all girls."

"Who was the Harbour Master?" we all asked to-gether.

"Li Po," said Aunt Effie. "I think he was Chinese."

"Are some of us descended from him?" asked Jazz.

"Probably," Aunt Effie replied. "What's your third name?"

"Abdul."

"Then you might be descended from the Arab slave trader I married on a bicycle trip through Africa."

"What's a Harbour Master?" asked Lizzie.

"Li Po's job was to keep the harbour ship-shape. He

saw my stacks of timber on the beach and asked what I was doing with them. I had to think fast.

"'I'm building a scow.'

"'That's all right, then,' he said, 'but you'd better get on with it.'

"I told him I couldn't start building it till the timber was properly seasoned," said Aunt Effie, "but he didn't hear a word I said. Li Po, the handsome Harbour Master, had fallen in love with me at first sight. He burst into tears at my beauty and swept me off my feet. Besides, I admired his uniform that had gold rings up both sleeves to the elbows. So I married him and remembered all I'd learned about boat-building from your Hindu great-great-great-great-grandfather and started building a scow."

"What's a scow?" asked Lizzie.

"What does it sound like?"

"Like a cow," said Lizzie, "with an s in front of it."

"We really must do something about your education," said Aunt Effie. "I lost my chance on the raft, but it's never too late to start."

"What were the names of your three daughters? The ones you had with Li Po?" asked Jane.

"I was so busy building the scow, I don't remember," said Aunt Effie, "but I suppose they must have had names. Those of you with straight black hair, you might be great-great-great-great-grandchildren of Li Po. Oh, he was handsome with his Harbour Master's uniform and his straight black hair. He could use chopsticks better than anyone I knew."

"I can use chopsticks!" David cried.

"You might be descended from him. And from me, of course! What a muddle!" Aunt Effie laughed. "Our family's a bit like the kauri we felled – or Humpty Dumpty. We couldn't put it together again now. Yet all the logs and planks came from the same tree."

Daisy and Johnny and Mabel and Flossie and Lynda and Stan and Howard and Marge and Stuart nodded as if they understood what she was saying. "Are we going to build a scow?" asked Lizzie, but just then a wind blew sand off the beach and into our faces. Eyes watering, we turned our backs to the wind. When we could see again, we were back home.

"I liked drifting down the river on the raft," Alwyn said as we milked the cows one day.

"I liked tripping the dam!" said Marie.

"I liked the arithmetic lessons," said Daisy.

"I want to build a scow," said Lizzie.

We all looked at each other. "Remember!" we said. And just then we heard Aunt Effie calling.

Note: *"Sprag, konaki, lace-bark, scow. I'm sure I won't be surprised if the little ones can't sleep tonight. It's all the fault of these difficult words."*
—Daisy.

Chapter Eight

Humpty, Dumpty, and the Hermit of Mangrove Island

Before Aunt Effie had finished calling our names, we were up on her bed. She shivered in her green canvas invalid's pyjamas and groaned, "I am dying, Egypt, dying."

"Who's Egypt?" asked Lizzie.

"A country round the other side of the world," Daisy said smartly.

"Can we go to Egypt?"

"You'd need a boat."

"Couldn't Aunt Effie take us there?"

"Only if she had a boat."

"Aunt Effie's built lots of boats!" said Lizzie.

Aunt Effie opened her eyes, looked at Lizzie, at Daisy, and back at Lizzie, and coughed deep and slow like a dying cow. "The fire's going out," she moaned. "Light the fire, Casey-Lizzie-Jared-Jessie. Light the fire!" She pulled a pipe from under her pillow. Before she could light it, Daisy started coughing and waving her hands in front of her face.

"I think we might build a scow," Aunt Effie said. She sounded a bit better.

"Hooray!" we all shouted.

Aunt Effie blew her pipe. An enormous bubble bulged out of it and filled the room. We sat inside it as the walls of the bubble shivered red, blue, and green.

"Light the fire!" Aunt Effie's voice was stronger.

Lizzie slipped down, ran to the fireplace, and threw some tea-tree twigs on the ashes. There were a few tiny crackles. Thick smoke rose and – Poom! – exploded into flame. A sharp-smelling grey cloud rolled out of the fireplace and filled the inside of the bubble that burst – Bang! – as Lizzie jumped for the bed. Aunt Effie's room vanished and the rest of us were standing on the beach at the mouth of the Mangrove River, by the stacks of timber. There was a thud and Lizzie, one eyebrow singed, landed in the sand beside us.

"Hello!" she said.

"Daisy-Mabel-Johnny-Flossie-Lynda-Stan-Howard-Marge-Stuart! Marie-Peter-Colleen-Alwyn-Bryce-Jack! Ann-Jazz-Becky-Jane-Isaac-David-Victor! Casey-Lizzie-Jared-Jess!" Aunt Effie shouted. We ran this way and that, dragging posts, digging holes, building trestles as she ordered.

We adzed square some kauri beams Aunt Effie called kelsons. When we'd finished spiking planks across them, she nodded and said, "That's the bottom of the hull."

"You'd think the planks would go on fore and aft," said Peter who seemed to know what we were building. Aunt Effie grinned and said nothing.

We left a broad slot in the middle. "For the centre-case," she said, and Peter nodded.

"Centre-case?" Daisy asked in her most unpleasant voice. "Fore and aft? Kelsons? We don't even know what we're building. What's a scow?"

"Remember what I said when we chopped down the kauri?" Aunt Effie looked at Daisy. "If you have to have every word explained to you, then you'll never get anything done. Write them all down and put them in your glossary at the back of the book."

She turned to the rest of us. "We want a good coat of tar on these planks. And then you can caulk the cracks between them with oakum."

"Caulk!' said Daisy writing busily. "Oakum!"

"The oakum's like the bookau when we waterproofed the dam," said Jared. He drove the oakum into the cracks between the planks.

"Much the same!" said Aunt Effie. "Watch out for your fingers with that caulking hammer."

"Ow!"

"You drive the oakum in," said Aunt Effie. "Not your fingers."

"Where does oakum come from?" asked Ann. She held up a handful of the fibres.

"It's just old ropes. Unpicked in the dark by convicts in cold caves under Mount Eden Prison in Auckland."

Bryce and Colleen tried to unpick a short end of rope and tore their finger nails.

"That's what happens to the convicts. Their nails get torn, and their fingertips wear down. I've seen the poor devils with fingers worn down past the first knuckles from picking oakum." Aunt Effie showed us what she meant on her hands, and Daisy gasped.

"If it's rope," said Casey, "why is it black?"

"They're old ships' ropes coated in Stockholm tar. It preserves the caulking, helps make it watertight."

We painted the caulked planks with tar again, and covered them with a layer of tarred felt. "To help keep out the worm," said Aunt Effie. "The worm doesn't eat you," she told the little ones. "So there's no need to paint yourselves."

"What's that?" Daisy held her nose and pointed at a barrel.

"Whale oil." Aunt Effie poured it into a bigger barrel. She added shell lime. We knew it was made from burnt shells. "Stir this!"

When it was well mixed, Aunt Effie said, "Now it's called schenam!"

We poured the schenam on top of the tarred felt that covered the caulked and tarred planks. "It's like thick cream!" said Jessie as the little ones spread it.

"Great stuff, schenam," said Aunt Effie, "for keeping out the worm!"

"Worm, schenam," said Daisy writing fast.

Last of all, we sheathed the bottom with totara planks running fore and aft. "I see," said Peter.

"Totara lasts better than most," said Aunt Effie. "It's tough, and it helps keep out the worm." But we caulked and tarred the cracks between the totara planks as well.

"Kelsons, planks, oakum caulking, felt, schenam, totara sheathing," said Peter. "It makes a strong bottom."

Aunt Effie nodded. "Don't forget the tar!"

"If a scow's a ship," said Jessie, why didn't we put down a keel and fix a stem and a stern-post to it, the way Captain Flash built his frigate?"

We all looked at Aunt Effie. "You'll see," she said. "A scow's like no other ship! Come on – we'll need to make shear-legs and whims if we're going to turn her over."

The shear-legs were made out of three kauri rickers lashed together at the top, their feet wide apart. What Aunt Effie called a block, but we knew as a pulley, hung from the lashing. There were two sets of shear-legs.

Behind each set we built a whim. They looked just like a ship's capstans. "I know what they're for!" said Casey. "I've read about them. They're for winding ropes and lifting anchors."

"Shear-legs, blocks, whim, capstan," wrote Daisy.

Aunt Effie and Marie fastened wire ropes to the whims and ran them up over the blocks and down under the bottom of the hull with its kelsons, planks, caulking, felt, schenam, totara sheathing, caulking, and tar. It looked too big to be shifted, let alone turned over.

We poured hot fat on the necks of the whims, to make the drums turn easily. Then we each took a short pole and pushed it into a slot in the head of a whim. Marie was helping Aunt Effie. Daisy was busy writing words she didn't understand. So there were twelve of us to a whim.

"Heave ho, my hearties, heave!" Aunt Effie sang out. We heaved on our poles. The whims turned. The wire ropes took up the strain. One side of the bottom lifted slowly. "Heave, ho!" It lifted further. "Heave, ho!"

Aunt Effie and Marie scrambled up and refastened the ropes so the bottom wouldn't go over with a bang. Slowly, we turned our whims and lowered it the other way up. While Peter took off the wire ropes, the rest of us scrambled all over it.

"It's very flat!" we all said. "It's huge, Aunt Effie. Where are the ribs?"

But she was busy showing us how to saw bent pohutukawa branches for the knees. "I suppose you'd call them the ribs," said Peter. "There's not going to be much room below decks, Aunt Effie. Not enough to stand up!"

"Hold scows are too tender for my liking. They capsize too easily," said Aunt Effie. "We're building a deck scow. We'll carry all our cargo on deck."

"What are we going to carry?" asked Lizzie.

"Wait and see. Keep your eyes open, and you'll see something worth knowing; keep your ears open, and you'll hear something worth learning."

We kept our eyes open and learned through-bolts go right through two pieces of timber and are fastened at each end. We kept our ears open and learned the chine is where the bottom of the ship turns into the side. Peter ran his hand along its sharp angle and said, "That's what you call a hard chine." We planked and sheathed and caulked the sides and painted them. We learned the space of two or three feet between the deck and the bottom of the hull was called the bilges. Daisy wrote down chine and bilges.

"Keep your bilges dry," Aunt Effie said, "pump them out, and you're safe. If there's a bit of a blow, or your cargo shifts, any water in your bilges rushes across to the lee side. The side away from the windward – the weather side. That's when your flat bottom loses its grip, its suction – your lee chine goes down, your weather chine comes up, and over you go!"

We talked about bilges and lee and weather sides and the advantages of centre-boards over lee-boards. By now, Daisy knew more about the strange words than the rest of us put together. When she told Aunt Effie she was putting the chain-plates in the wrong position, Brutus bit Daisy's behind, and she had to sleep face-down that night.

One evening, we carried out the kedge anchor on the back of the dinghy. The new coir rope floated behind. Next morning, as the tide rose, we knocked out the blocks on the seaward side so the trestles under the scow sloped towards the water. From the whims we ran ropes out through snatch blocks fastened to deadmen – big posts dug into the sand at low tide. We pushed on the arms, the ropes lifted and pulled. The pawls clicked on the ship's capstan as we heaved on the kedge, and the scow slid sideways.

"She's afloat!" Peter cried.

"Sixty-six feet nine inches by eighteen feet six inches, and so she should – she's the amazing scow! She'll lift in less water than it takes to float a mangrove berry," said Aunt Effie. "Centre-board up, she'll skim across a pipi bank on a heavy dew. She'll sail on the froth and scum on top of the mud before the tide comes in. She'll slide up a mangrove creek where you'd never get a boat with a keel. And she'll sail all the way to Sydney fully-loaded with only a foot of freeboard, and a thousand fathoms of blue water beneath her!"

Aunt Effie held up a black bottle. "Old Puckeroo Extra Strong Scotch Gruel for Stiff Back, Baldness, Rhinitis, and Tonsillitis. Good for Women's and Horses' Ailments. Also Good for Men," she read off the label. "Good for scows, too!" She pulled the cork out with her teeth, swigged several times, rammed the cork back in, whirled the bottle around her head, and smashed it over the shapely bow. "I name you *Margery Daw*!

"Pick up the broken glass, Daisy," she added. "We don't want anyone cutting their bare feet."

That afternoon we rigged shear-legs on the deck, ran a rope through a block hanging from them, and stepped the mizzen-mast. With that rigged, we had no trouble raising the foremast.

We learned to splice – both short and long splices on wire and Manila rope. We took the hardwood deadeyes we'd carved and shackled one end to the chain-plates. We rove the greased lanyards through the other holes in the deadeyes and heaved the shrouds down to stay the masts. We crawled and swung and climbed and rigged the ship, all the standing and then all the running rigging.

We learned the difference between Manila and coir rope. How coir floats and stretches when wet, so it's handy for mooring in a surge. We learned the difference between sheet, bower, and kedge anchors. We said over and over again: "Kedge, bower, sheet. Coir, manila. Stay, shroud, deadeye, lanyard, standing and running rigging, mizzen, fore and aft." And Daisy scribbled words into her glossary.

We ran out the jib-boom. We bent on the sails. A few days later, topmasts sent up, the great barn-door of a rudder fixed on its gudgeons, every tackle chock-a-block, we skimmed across the pipi banks on an incoming tide. In those days, the Mangrove River was much wider, and it took several weeks to reach the channel. Under Whitianga Rock we turned and ran upstream.

"River trials," said Aunt Effie.

A few more weeks, and we were standing to and fro off Quarry Point. We'd adjusted and refastened every bit of standing rigging. We were getting good at handling the *Margery Daw*.

"Time we had a bit of fun," said Aunt Effie.

Either side of the bows, there was something humped and hard and secret and covered in green canvas. Aunt Effie stripped off the tarpaulins. Crouched grinning in wickedness, two brass chasers gaped through their gun ports, one either side of the bowsprit. The starboard cannon had Humpty engraved on it. The other was called Dumpty. We ran them in and loaded the cartridges of powder, the nine-pound balls, and tamped the wads home. We heaved on the gun-tackles, and ran up both guns.

Aunt Effie glanced along Humpty's barrel and tapped a wedge as Marie steered toward Mangrove Island. "It's called a quoin," She said, tapping the wedge. We used our eyes and saw it raised the barrel. Daisy wrote "quoin" in her glossary.

On the white sandbank at the head of Mangrove Island, somebody had built a hut, tall enough to stand in, but too small to turn around in. "It looks like somebody's dunny," said Jessie.

Aunt Effie glanced along the top of Humpty's barrel again, lifted the elevation a shade, took the smoking slow-match from its tub and blew on it. One last look along the barrel and she gave the slow-match to Lizzie who plunged it on the powder in the touch-hole.

"Boom!" Humpty leapt back and was brought up by the gun-tackle. The dunny roof blew off. A squawk echoed the boom, as a doubled-up figure shot out of the door and disappeared over the sandbank. Lizzie capered, black with smoke and reeking of gunpowder.

As Marie swung the *Margery Daw* back on course, Aunt Effie clapped a speaking-trumpet to her mouth. "That'll teach you to leave my spuds alone!" she shouted.

There was another squawk from the island, as we swabbed out Humpty's smoking barrel with a mop.

We didn't dare ask Aunt Effie what was going on. Not even Lizzie and Jessie spoke. Daisy stood looking disapproving as Aunt Effie conned the ship past the tail of Mangrove Island and up past Hamilton's Point. At last, Daisy took a deep breath but, before she could say anything, Aunt Effie asked, "Have you ever seen anyone fired out of a cannon?" and Daisy swallowed her breath and didn't dare say a word.

We ran up and down the ratlines. We took our tricks at the brass-bound steering wheel, spinning its mahogany spokes. We climbed out the bowsprit, right out on the jib-boom. Some of us fell and shoved each other over the side, and we caught hold of ropes and clambered back aboard. Lizzie wouldn't swim because she didn't want to lose the grime of cannon smoke and the smell of gunpowder. We slid between the mangroves, wound up the creeks to the Kaimarama and up the Waiwawa to the tide-water booms. Several months later, when the wind came round and blew from the south, we kedged the scow around in a puddle of fresh water only half her length, and sailed back down the river.

As we drove past Mangrove Island, Aunt Effie ran out Dumpty, the brass chaser on the port bow. "You wouldn't believe it!" she said. "He's rebuilt his dunny in the same place! Stand clear," she ordered Jessie, "or you'll lose your feet when Old Dumpty recoils."

Peter held the *Margery Daw* steady. Auntie Effie handed Jessie the slow-match. "Boom!" Smoke rolled across the water. Dumpty leapt back and was brought up by the tackle. The dunny flew to pieces. We saw the cannon-ball skip on top of the sandbank and take the roof off a nikau whare behind. Somebody squawked.

One hand on a stay, one foot on the bulwark, Auntie

Effie shouted through the speaking- trumpet. "And you can leave my kumaras alone, too!"

There was another squawk from the island, and we were past.

"That hermit," said Aunt Effie, "he thinks he can help himself to my vegie garden below Hamilton's Point any time he likes. Last time I went for a feed, he'd dug up a couple of rows of spuds. And he'd been into my kumara pit. I could tell it was him by the shape of his footprints in the dirt."

Note: *"Really! If you want to know what a word means, you'll just have to look it up in the glossary. Why can't you just do what I do? Listen to Aunt Effie, and most of the words make sense anyway. So there!"* —Daisy.

Chapter Nine

Sea Trials and a Good Stow

Mangrove Island sank in our wake. A few weeks' run down the river, we swept past Mr Browne's stone jetty on the eastern side, closed Cemetery Point behind, and felt the *Margery Daw* lift to the swell.

"Now for her sea trials!" said Aunt Effie.

The *Margery Daw* worked out past Centre Island as the wind went around into the north. We wedged the centre-board to stop it thumping in its case.

Marie was struggling with the wheel. "She keeps wanting to turn up into the wind," she said.

"Too much weather helm." Aunt Effie lowered the rudder a bit more. "How's that?" Marie smiled and nodded back.

Just then Lizzie came out with the question we'd all been wanting to ask. "What shape are the footprints of the hermit of Mangrove Island?" she asked.

"Small and narrow!" said Aunt Effie. "An elegant foot with a remarkably high instep – for a man, that is. He used to dance divinely, but he's been deaf for years now and can't hear the music. It's a wonder he even heard our cannon."

Daisy clicked her tongue disapprovingly: "Tsk! Tsk! Tsk!" We all knew what she was thinking.

Off the Whauwhau, the anchor went down through water so clear we saw sand kick up as the flukes bit. We struck the topmasts, sailed inside the cave at Waiatai, and saw a huge fin sink in the black water. The only sounds were a drip from the roof and our beating hearts.

Aunt Effie put the speaking-trumpet to her mouth, hummed like a bull moaning, and the black water moved. A huge head came up, a giant eye looked at us and sank slowly out of sight.

The roof was so high we sent up the topmasts again and explored the rest of the cave. After several days' sailing in the dark, the cave finished in a rusty iron door. In the light from the hurricane lanterns hung in the rigging, we saw the word "Danger!" and a skull and crossbones painted in red.

"Give it a fright," Aunt Effie told Lizzie, and gave her the speaking-trumpet.

"You mustn't blow through that thing," Daisy warned Lizzie. "It'll taste of ear wax!"

Lizzie blew a screeching wail, but the door stayed shut. Daisy shook her head.

"How about a shot from Humpty and Dumpty?" asked Jessie.

"Not inside the cave. The noise would blow out our eardrums," said Aunt Effie. "We'll come back some day with a crowbar." She brought the *Margery Daw* about, and we sailed for the mouth of the cave. Even with the topmasts struck, the mainmast cap scraped the roof. The tide had come in. We had to wait inside the cave overnight for it to drop again before we could get out and, all that dark time, we felt something looking at us.

It was good being back in the sunlight. We spent several months cruising between the Mercury Islands and the Aldermans then turned and ran in to Purangi, lifting the centre-board and rudder, astonishing a shark sunbathing in a couple of feet of water on the bar, and beached with a soft crunch of shells on a pipi bank up the river.

"We've just got time to raid old Harry Wigmore's orchard," said Aunt Effie. But Mr Wigmore chased us off with a blunderbuss, so we had a feed of oysters off the rocks below old Mrs Ross's cottage and raided her orchard instead.

For tea we ate pipis and young mullet steamed on top of a kerosene tin of new potatoes. As the *Margery Daw* stirred and lifted next morning on the incoming tide, we ate flounder for breakfast. Afterwards, Aunt Effie disappeared and popped out of the cabin wearing her long-legged, long-sleeved, high-necked, green canvas swimming costume. She pulled on a bathing cap that made her head look like a hydrangea.

"You're not swimming straight after a meal!" Daisy spoke darkly. "I know a little girl who did, and she sank straight to the bottom."

"Nonsense!" Aunt Effie dived into the river, climbed

on amidships where there were no bulwarks, and went to dive again. "It's lovely! Why don't you come in?"

"We're scared," Jessie told her. "We painted the bottom with tar and schenam so the worm wouldn't eat it. What if it eats us?"

"Yes," said Lizzie. "Shouldn't you paint us with tar before we get in the water?"

"Nonsense! The teredo worm eats only wood." She dived in again. Her hydrangea head popped up, and we all whooped and dived in after her. All except Daisy who sat digesting her meal for at least an hour

After several weeks swimming, fishing, and picnicking along Cooks Beach, Lonely Bay, Colvilles Beach, and Front Beach, we tacked up the Mangrove River and moored alongside the boom in Back Bay. Aunt Effie hooted through the speaking-trumpet until the echoes bounced off Whitianga Rock.

"We've got a few adjustments to make to the rigging," she said, "before you see what sort of a cargo she'll carry." She jumped into the shrouds and ran up the ratlines to examine the mizzen tressel.

"I'm sure that's Captain Flash's ear-trumpet. She said he died years ago, but he must be the hermit of Mangrove Island!" Even though Daisy hissed them, we could hear her words clearly.

There was another hiss – from Aunt Effie's hands – as she landed on the deck beside Daisy. "What's that?" she asked, hands still smoking from coming down the backstay so fast.

"That Captain Flash," Daisy spoke up. "You said he

died of disappointment, hundreds of years ago."

"Perhaps I got it wrong," said Aunt Effie. "You'll find it pays not to worry too much about time, Daisy. Like distances. When you grow up, it'll only take a couple of days to get to Auckland from the Bay. Now it takes several months or a couple of years. But it's more fun, taking longer. I always think time and distance are much the same.

"Captain Flash?" she said in a thrilling voice. "I sometimes think it was his uniform I fell in love with. When I try to picture him all I see is gold epaulettes, silver spurs, medals, and a bugle – no it's his ear-trumpet I'm seeing. Mind you, he was a wonderful dancer! Of course he lost his looks when his head went pointed. His eyes squinted, and his ears were all sort of crushed against the side of his skull."

"You said you married him." Daisy gave a proper little sniff.

"So I did, but that dissolute missionary, the Reverend Samuel, got the words wrong so the marriage wasn't legal. Captain Flash was inconsolable. That's probably why I said he died of disappointment. And then I went on to marry the wretched missionary himself, or Rangi the Maori chief. One or other or perhaps all of them.

"Whenever you speak, dear," Aunt Effie told Daisy, "I think I'm listening to Captain Flash again. He had a loud, penetrating voice that carried well. Everyone said he would have made a good teacher. Captain Flash was probably your great-great-great-great-grandfather."

We knew Daisy wouldn't like that! She liked to say

she was descended from a missionary. She swallowed, and tried to keep quiet, but her mouth popped open and she said, "It's against the law to marry more than one person. 'Accursed is the bigamist!'"

"What a proper little sea-lawyer you are, Daisy," said Aunt Effie. "No, don't bite her, Brutus."

"Besides, how is Captain Flash alive if he died of disappointment all those years ago?" Daisy asked and gave a shriek.

"Brutus! I'm very disappointed in you! I don't know the answer to that question," Aunt Effie nodded to Daisy. "Perhaps you'd better ask the hermit yourself. Only don't call him Captain Flash. He doesn't like it, for some reason." She leapt as she spoke, grabbed Daisy by the scruff of her neck, swung her into the dinghy, and shoved her off. The tide was racing in and carried the dinghy away up the river.

"Now," said Aunt Effie, "we can have another look at our rig. When you're coming about on a big schooner, a three-masted one, you have to haul the topsails down on the fore and main caps, put the helm down, haul the head sheets over then, once you're on the other tack, climb up and dip the halliards over the jumper stay and topmast forestay and reset the topsails."

Peter nodded. Perhaps he understood what she was talking about. The rest of us were watching Daisy disappearing past the end of Whitianga Rock, putting in the rowlocks, running out the oars, and still shrieking in her carrying voice.

"Of course," said Aunt Effie, "your schooner rig

carries a bigger spread of canvas – the extra height of the mainmast. And a schooner's masts are stayed better: you don't often see a schooner's topmast carried away, whereas a ketch's … well, in a ketch the whole of the pull of the headsails is taken on the foremast.

"Still, overall, I prefer the ketch rig. You can manage with a smaller crew. Maybe it doesn't work up to windward quite as well, but that's not what scows are for."

"What are scows for?" asked Jessie.

"I'll show you when Daisy gets back." All the time she'd been talking, Aunt Effie had been making adjustments to the rigging. Late that afternoon, as we swung out the heavy lifting gear, a strong pole fastened to the foot of the foremast, Daisy came rowing down on the outgoing tide.

"Did you see the hermit?" cried Aunt Effie.

"He wore a tall black top hat, so I couldn't see his head. When I asked if he was Captain Flash, he put one hand to his ear and told me to speak up. Then when I did, he called me a rude name." Daisy's face went red as she climbed aboard. "Then some Maori kids came past in a canoe, selling peaches."

"They'll be some of your cousins," said Aunt Effie.

Daisy pretended not to hear. "The hermit called them rude names too, so one whipped out a shanghai, and knocked off his hat with a hard green peach. Before he could put it back on, I saw his eyes were squinty, his ears folded over, and his head went up to a point. The kids paddled away shouting, 'Te Pointy! Te Pointy!'"

"He never was good with children, your great-great-

great-great-grandfather."

"He might have a high instep," Daisy said in her most dignified voice, "but he said some very vulgar things when the Maori kids called him Te Pointy. I'm sure he's not my great-great-great-great-grandfather!"

"Daisy-Mabel-Johnny-Flossie-Lynda-Stan-Howard-Marge-Stuart! Lead this rope around the capstan," Aunt Effie said, changing the subject. "Peter-Marie-Colleen-Alwyn-Bryce-Jack! Open the boom. Ann-Jazz-Becky-Jane-Isaac-David-Victor! Pole that log alongside. Now, Casey, Lizzie, Jared, Jess, slip the strop around it. That's the way."

We heaved on the capstan, the heavy lifting gear groaned, the pawls clicked, the rope came in, and the great log rolled streaming up the side of the *Margery Daw*, and on to the deck.

"So that's why we've got no bulwarks amidships," said Peter, but Aunt Effie was already working the log forward. The steel toes of her timber-jack dug into the false deck she'd insisted we lay. Everything was beginning to make sense.

The logs were too heavy for us to lift, but they parbuckled up the side no trouble. When the scow tilted to port, we started loading from starboard.

"Chock them well," said Aunt Effie. "There's nothing worse than a loose log, unless it's a loose cannon."

"Do you mean cannon can get loose?" asked Lizzie.

"They've smashed more than a few ships to pieces. Best thing is to sway cannon down below before a storm."

"But we've got no hold," said Jessie.

"So ours have to stay where they are," Aunt Effie told her. "It's a minor disadvantage of a deck scow, that you can't strike your cannon down below."

We drove in the chocks. Parbuckling chains went right around the logs as well. When they covered the deck from the foremast to the mizzen, we dragged up still more and chained them on top.

"A good stow is important," said Aunt Effie. "There's nothing worse than having your cargo move at sea, unless it's having a fire."

The logs now hid much of the scow. Jared and Jessie fell overboard, climbed back on and said, "We've got hardly any freeboard!"

"We don't need much," said Aunt Effie. "With a load of kauri, we're not going to sink. And as long as we pump our bilges, we won't go over, not if we handle her properly. The cargo's pressing down, and the water's pressing up. So the heavier the load, the tighter your deck scow's pressed together. In a hold scow, the cargo tends to push the ship apart."

Lizzie looked a bit unsure what Aunt Effie meant and jumped up and down a couple of times on the top logs.

"We'll have to put a log-reef in the mainsail," said Aunt Effie, "or the boom won't clear those ones you're jumping on."

A southerly drift filling our topsails, we cast off at midnight to catch the tide, and slipped down the Mangrove River in the dark. Out we went past Centre Island, past

Opito, through the passage inside Mercury Island. A couple of months later, constant head winds made us run into Kennedy Bay.

Note: "If you don't know a word, look it up in the glossary! And don't swim straight after a meal or you'll go straight to the bottom." —Daisy.

Chapter Ten

How the Horse Latitudes Got their Name

"*We should be* grateful for those head winds," said Aunt Effie as the cable rattled out in Kennedy Bay. "We're a bit light on tucker for crossing the Hauraki Gulf, and I know a couple of good snapper possies in here. While we're about it, we can salt down some wild pork."

"How big is the Gulf?"

"Just around the corner from Cape Colville and between Cape Rodney, the Great Barrier, and the Little Barrier, there's the Horse Latitudes," Aunt Effie told Lizzie. "Then there's the North-East Trade Wind, then the Doldrums. Once we're across the Equator and out of them, we'll pick up the South-East Trades that should carry us all the way into Auckland There are quicker ways of crossing the Gulf, but – like I said before – not as much fun."

"What are the Horse Latitudes?"

"Several centuries ago, a shipful of Aussie bookies and touts was crossing from Sydney with a load of no-hoper

nags their owners were going to fill with drugs to make them win the Auckland Cup. They ran into calms as they entered the Gulf. After several months with slack sails, sudden thunderstorms, and no wind, they ran short of water. The captain ordered the bookies and touts thrown overboard. They swam ashore and became our first members of parliament. Still it didn't rain, so the captain ordered the horses thrown overboard."

"Poor horses!" Lizzie wept loudly.

"The captain died of scurvy, but the intelligent horses learned to tread water and keep their mouths wide-open when it rained. They had plenty to drink and developed a taste for seaweed. Once the salt water rusted away their heavy iron horseshoes, they got pretty good at breast-stroke. They grew longer tails, used their ears as fins, and learned how to duck-dive and hold their breath under water. Soon it was hard to tell the sea horses from the dolphins. They may not be able to swim quite as fast but, being horses, they can jump a lot higher. That's how you tell a sea horse from a dolphin."

Lizzie dried her eyes and nodded.

"When Poseidon, the World King of the Horses, heard

what those Aussies had done, he put a curse on them," said Aunt Effie. "That's why Waharoa horses always win the Melbourne Cup. The Aussie trainers call it the King's Curse. And ever since then, that belt of sea above the North-East Trades has been called the Horse Latitudes."

Aunt Effie looked through her telescope at the bush behind the beach. "There's fresh rooting in the pig-fern on that ridge," she said and put the dogs away. Caligula, Nero, Brutus, Kaiser, Genghis, and Boris picked up the first good wave and surfed in standing up. Having four feet, dogs don't need a surfboard. Whooping and baying, they disappeared through the sandhills. As we rowed towards a rock where Aunt Effie said we'd catch snapper, she called, "I don't trust the dogs with matches. You'll have to give them a hand singeing the pigs."

We caught several dinghy-loads of snapper and built a smokehouse on the beach. The only other building in the bay was a church leaning against a stack of empty bottles at which Daisy pointed disapprovingly. A well-spoken old gentleman came out, and we gave him half a dozen of our fattest fish. He thanked us in a courteous voice, and asked the name of our scow.

"The *Margery Daw*," we told him. "We built her."

"In my youth," said the well-spoken old gentleman, "I knew a young woman who built a thirty-two gun frigate."

"Our aunt once built a thirty-two gun frigate."

"Great Scott! And what, may I ask, was its name?" The well-spoken old gentleman trembled, and we noticed his breath smelled of strong liquor.

"The *Dainty Ankle!*" we told the old gentleman who was now hiccuping and spitting with excitement.

"By Jove! And what did you say your aunt's name is?"

"Aunt Effie."

"Astounding!" The well-spoken old gentleman shaded his eyes with a shaking hand and stared out to the scow where Aunt Effie was sunbathing on top of the bowsprit in a green canvas bikini. "Effie!" His voice shook. "I wonder could that possibly be short for Euphemia?"

Just then the dogs came down through the sandhills, each with a gigantic boar flung over its back. They threw the carcasses down, snarled, and menaced us. Daisy looked white and squeaked: "Give them the matches!"

Fortunately, Marie was built of sterner stuff. She lit some tea-tree with a single match, threw ponga fronds on the flames, and produced a dense white smoke. The boars were too big for us to shift, so we felled some rickers, threw up shear-legs, and suspended the carcasses over the fire. The flames and moist smoke singed and loosened the bristles, and we scraped them off with mussel shells. By that time, the dogs had returned with another six boars.

"Think of all the roast pork crackling!" said Jared.

We offered some chops to the well-spoken old gentleman, but he was talking to himself and shuffling in circles on the sandhills. As we rowed out the last of the carcasses to the *Margery Daw*, we heard him singing, "Come Into the Garden, Euphemia!" a very popular song when he was a young man, so he had told us.

We swung up the carcasses with the heavy lifting gear and hung them in the rigging, their white tusks clashing like cutlasses as the scow rose and fell. Altogether we put down three-score barrels of salt junk, and smoked five tons of snapper.

"That should see us across the Gulf – with any luck," said Aunt Effie. "Good dogs!" she told Caligula, Nero, Brutus, Kaiser, Genghis, and Boris who whacked the deck with their tails and licked her hands as she stitched up their rips and wounds with her sacking needle.

The wind had come around. We tripped the anchor and got the cable straight up and down. "Did I hear singing from the beach?" Aunt Effie asked as we heaved on the capstan. Too breathless to speak, we nodded as we catted the anchor, hauled on the halliards, got the headsails pulling, winched up the heavy mainsail and mizzen, set the topsails, and stowed the last of the snapper. The scow was already sailing fast past Black Nancy's Point when we got our breath back and told Aunt Effie about the well-spoken old gentleman.

"He was singing a very pretty song called, 'Come Into the Garden, Eu-something or other,'" said Daisy.

"Was he, indeed?"

Daisy gave a knowing little smile. "He said he once knew a young woman who built a thirty-two gun frigate."

"Indeed!"

"He's a very respectable old gentleman," said Daisy. "He lives in a church." Aunt Effie said nothing. Daisy prattled on. "He'd forgotten his own name, but he wondered if yours was Eu–"

But before Daisy could say the name, she fell over as Aunt Effie put down the helm. The scow came about smartly, and we made quick time back into Kennedy Bay. "I'll teach him to call me names!" Aunt Effie muttered as she opened the ports, hauled on the gun tackles, and ran out our brass chasers.

"I hope you're not going to blow up the church?"

"No, Daisy. I'm just going to make his ears ring a bit." Aunt Effie squinted along the top of Humpty's barrel, and fired. DING! The bell in the church steeple rang very loudly. The well-spoken old gentleman ran out, fingers in his ears.

"How dare you say my name is Euphemia?" Aunt Effie shouted through her speaking-trumpet as she fired Dumpty. This time the bell rang DONG!

"My name is Effie!" she bellowed. "And don't you forget it!"

We could still hear the bells ringing DING! DONG! as we stood north off Waikawau. In fact they rang so loudly – DING! DONG! – the echoes kept coming out of the gullies behind Kennedy Bay for several years.

"That abominable missionary," said Aunt Effie, "he's the one who got the words wrong when he married me."

She gave us the course to clear Te Anaputa Point, and we saw Daisy go to say something. Fortunately, Peter called her to give him a hand closing the gun ports and polishing Humpty and Dumpty before lashing their tarpaulins over them. He said quietly, "Perhaps you'd better not ask Aunt Effie if her name is really Euphemia."

"Why not, if it's true?"

"She doesn't seem to like it," Peter told her.

"Huh!" Daisy tossed her head.

"Do you really want to get bitten again?"

Caligula, Nero, and Brutus had followed Daisy up to the foredeck and surrounded her, slurping and champing. Daisy swallowed. We were all relieved when she said nothing more.

We rounded Cape Colville, passed inside the Watchman with its wooden clatter of nesting gannets, and entered the Hauraki Gulf. Aunt Effie waved one hand at the kauri logs, the blue water, the curved sails above our heads.

"Fully laden, and all of twelve knots. This is what a scow's for!" she told Jessie.

"Peter, just let her head drop off a point. We'll make up more in speed than we'll lose in leeway." Aunt Effie turned away, saying to herself, "Never jam a scow on the wind."

"Where are the Doldrums?" Casey asked.

"Sometimes they're as far north as the Three Kings. Sometimes as far south as the Happy Jacks. It just depends. Some people say they're just a state of mind."

"I'm cold," said Jessie, and the other little ones complained.

"Better put on your oilskins and sou'westers. We're going to see a bit of fog." Before Aunt Effie finished speaking, the jib-boom vanished. The bowsprit and headsails disappeared. The foremast and mainsail were hidden in a white wall that rushed along the deck and over the logs towards us.

Suddenly everything dripped wet and cold. We felt for the shrouds, ran up the ratlines, shinned up the top-masts, and stuck our heads out of the dense fog into bright sunshine. Lizzie and Casey took off their oilskins and sou'westers and threw them down on top of the fog. It was so thick they jumped and ran across it. The harder they jumped, the higher they bounced. Some-where down below, Aunt Effie's voice called, "If the fog thins you'll fall through." Casey and Lizzie shrieked and scrambled back on to the topmast as their oilskins slid sideways down a hole in the fog.

"That could have happened to you," said Daisy.

We were working out our position by the peaks of the Little Barrier, the Great Barrier, and the crest of Moehau when, sticking out of the fog and coming straight for us, we saw the black topsails of a three-masted scow, schooner-rigged. Aunt Effie came up and had a look herself.

"It's that black-hearted pirate," she said, "who mooches around between Colville and Cape Rodney, looking for loaded scows to plunder. 'Plucking the Pakeha!' he calls it. Quiet now. If he hears us, he'll make us all walk the plank. Get down on deck, hold on to your tongues, and don't make a sound!"

"What does walk the plank mean?" asked Jessie, but Aunt Effie pulled a face, poked out her tongue, grabbed hold of it, and we all copied her so we couldn't make a sound. With our other hands we held the dogs' tongues so they couldn't bark. We all took a deep breath and held it.

As we bore away toward the invisible Coromandel

coast, somebody coughed. We looked round-eyed at
Aunt Effie and shook our heads. It must have been one
of the pirates. Then we heard him spit. Aunt Effie stared
to starboard where the fog was even thicker, and something shifted in it. Something darker than the fog. We
listened and heard the hiss and slice of the pirate's
cutwater and people saying words we weren't allowed
to use.

"Fore and main tops'ls down!" The voice was so close
we could have touched it. We heard the run of halliards,
the creak of blocks.

"Fore and main tops'ls down, Cap'n!" a voice cried.

"Put your helm down!" we heard the pirate captain
tell the man on the wheel. "Down, curse you!" And we
heard a blow.

"Ow!" came out of the fog, and the clink of rudder
chains. Aunt Effie shook her head.

"Haul those head sheets over!" the bold voice cried,
sounding fainter now as the schooner-rigged scow drew
away on the other tack.

Lizzie pointed up into the fog where our own topsails, we knew, were shining in the sun, but Aunt Effie
shook her head. We would have to take the risk of the
pirates seeing them.

There came another distant roar. We stared afraid at
Aunt Effie. She smiled as well as she could while holding her tongue with one hand and the wheel with the
other.

Aunt Effie let go her tongue and swallowed. "He's
sending them up to dip the halliards over the jumper

stay and topmast forestay," she whispered. "Like I told you. With any luck, they'll be so busy resetting the topsails, they won't have time to look behind."

The rest of us let out our breaths. We'd been holding them so long, our ears and noses were pink.

"Up you go and see if you can spot him!"

North of west towards Cape Rodney, there was something that might have been the black topmasts of a pirate scow. They vanished as we slid down the backstays into the thick fog. But instead of landing back on the deck, we found ourselves sitting on the foot of Aunt Effie's enormous bed. Flop! Flop! Casey's and Lizzie's oilskins landed beside them.

Jessie grizzled, "I wanted to see the pirate," and Jared cried and said he wanted to keep sailing to Auckland, but a gruff voice asked, "Do you want to wake the Bugaboo?" and we leapt screaming on to the floor, and ran downstairs where there was roast pork and crackling and apple sauce for tea.

Note: *"See, I told you just to keep reading and you'd understand all the words. If you don't there's an excellent glossary at the back of the book"* —Daisy.

Chapter Eleven

Doldrums and Dancing Walruses

We were cleaning up the orchard for winter when Aunt Effie vanished, leaving her scythe hooked over a branch of an apple tree. Her green canvas invalid's pyjamas that had been airing in front of the fire disappeared. Daisy looked at once and reported that the bottle of Old Puckeroo Universal and Benevolent Knee Rub had gone off the mantelpiece.

As we pruned the row of asparagus trees beside the back door we heard Aunt Effie call: "Daisy-Mabel-Johnny-Flossie-Lynda-Stan-Howard-Marge-Stuart-Peter-Marie-Colleen-Alwyn-Bryce-Jack-Ann-Jazz-Becky-Jane-Isaac-David-Victor-Casey-Lizzie-Jared-Jess!"

We dropped our ladders, pruning knives, saws, secateurs, wheelbarrows, rakes, ropes, and long-handled loppers, bolted upstairs, flung ourselves on the foot of Aunt Effie's enormous bed, and she croaked, "I am dying, Egypt, dying."

Johnny clapped his hand over Daisy's mouth.

"Give me some painkiller and let me speak a little," said Aunt Effie, pointing at the bottle of Old Puckeroo. She swallowed noisily. "Oh, modern medical science is such a wonderful thing, I feel better already!" She took another swig, her hair crackled and stood on end, and smoke curled out of her nostrils.

Daisy sniffed. Brutus growled at her, and Aunt Effie said, "I dreamt we were sailing across the Gulf with a load of kauri logs." We all nodded so hard, the dogs pricked their ears and barked.

"Better put on your oilskins and sou'westers," Aunt Effie told Casey and Lizzie, and she shook the bottle of Old Puckeroo. Smoke poured out its neck, white, cold, and wet. Aunt Effie's pillows vanished. Then she disappeared into the whiteness. Then we couldn't see the bedposts.

"Up you go and see where we are!" cried Aunt Effie's voice. We heard a sound like a halliard slapping, stuck our hands into the cold white fog and felt the rigging, swung ourselves into the shrouds and ran up the ratlines to the top of the mast. Off to our right we could see sunshine.

"Turn right!" cried Lizzie.

"Starboard!" said Jared.

The steering chains rattled on the invisible rudder. The boom-jaws groaned. The centre-board creaked. Above our heads, the topsail swung across and filled. The fog thinned below our feet, and we saw the main tressel appear, the ratlines, and the lower mast. The deck and our cargo of kauri logs spread out below in sunshine. For a moment we'd all had the same eerie feeling of sailing along without a ship below us. Then somewhere we heard: Boom! Boom!

"Great guns!" Jessie whispered.

Boom! Boom! Victor pointed south-west to a faraway column of smoke that sagged downwind.

"Look behind!" David cried.

Out of the wall of fog astern a black jib-boom emerged, followed by a black bowsprit and the black headsails of the pirate scow. We turned and ran ahead of the wind, the *Margery Daw's* best point of sailing, let out the log-reef in our main, rigged bonnets over the topsails and watersails under the booms, but the pirate came closer. We set the main and mizzen wing and wing, but still he came on.

Aunt Effie glanced west. "That white smoke, that's from the post office at the mouth of the Puhoi River. They always light their fire with tea-tree about three o'clock, this time of year." She glanced east. "There's Moehau." She looked astern. "The eastern peak of Little Barrier over my right shoulder," she muttered. "That puts us off Bryce Head … opening Jackman Bay south of–" But we didn't hear any more because there was a puff of smoke from the pirate's bows, a bang, and the bonnet over the mizzen topsail blew into little strips of canvas.

"If he hits a backstay, we're goners," said Aunt Effie.

"Can't we shoot back?" asked Lizzie.

"We'd have to shift our chasers aft. That'd mean rigging the heavy lifting gear."

Daisy shrieked, "You're not going to just let that pirate shoot us to pieces?" There was a bigger puff of smoke from the pirate's bows. Two round holes appeared in the mizzen topsail. We heard a double bang.

"Ho! Ho! Ho!" The pirates were so close, we could hear them drawing the daggers from between their teeth to jeer. They shook their fists. Instead of a hand, one had a hook that he jerked at us horribly. Several had a black patch over one eye. Two had a piece of cardboard where their noses should have been. And one vicious-looking pirate with no hair had no ears either, just little pink tags left where the rest had been bitten off in a fight. Amidships a cheerful-looking cabin girl was whistling and turning the handle of a grindstone for several pirates to sharpen their cutlasses.

"Keep going," said Aunt Effie to herself. "There should be a dead white tree on top of a hill in Jackman Bay. Little Barrier astern. Kawau Island over there."

"How do you know it's Kawau?" asked Lizzie.

"You can see Governor Grey's giraffe feeding amongst the pohutukawas. Moehau east. Bryce Head just opening Jackman Bay…." Aunt Effie's voice trailed off.

A tall pirate ran out on the black bowsprit, a pistol in each hand, a bloodstained cutlass gripped between his powerful jaws. He could almost jump on to our stern.

"What a striking figure!" exclaimed Daisy. "And what a superb suntan!"

"Bring her up into the wind and strike your colours!" shouted the pirate captain.

Aunt Effie murmured, "Keep going…."

"Heave to or I'll blow you out of the water!"

"Hadn't you better do what he says?" asked Daisy.

"He does speak beautifully clear English!"

"How would you like to go over the side?" Aunt Effie asked Daisy. "Bring her up into the wind, Peter. Just a point."

"But the schooner can sail into the wind faster!"

"Do what I say!"

The schooner gained on us immediately.

"Up another point."

The schooner was now so close we were deafened by the din of pirates gnashing their cast-iron false teeth. Sparks flew and burnt tiny holes in our mizzen sail.

"Half of you on to the centre-board handle, the rest on the tackle behind the foremast," said Aunt Effie. "When I give the word, I want that centre-board up in a flash.

"There's the white tree opening!" she cried. "Centre-board up!" It shot up inside its case and, with nothing to hold her against the water, the *Margery Daw* made lee-way, skidding sideways over heaving beds of seaweed. The swell lowered, the weed opened like a parting in long hair. Pink and white sea anemones lined the rocky blade of a reef just below our flat bottom. There was a tearing rasp from the rudder that Aunt Effie hadn't time to raise, and we were over the reef and in green water again.

"Drop the centre-board!" We felt its bite as the *Margery Daw* straightened up.

Behind us, the pirate captain screamed 'Down helm! Rocks ahead!" His much bigger scow had three centre-boards. The one for'ard, the fin-board, smashed into the reef first. The bow went down, the stern kicked up. The pirate scow stopped so suddenly, the midships and stern rammed up inside the bow like a telescope closing.

The pirate captain, his two for'ard chasers, and half his crew and their cutlasses with the cheerful-looking cabin girl catapulted into the seaweed. We cheered and the dogs barked as his fore and main masts broke off, tottered like trees falling, and thumped over to leeward, a fine tangle of rigging and canvas.

We pulled up our centre-board and slid back over the reef. Safe from the pirate's broadside because his gun ports were under water, we dropped our centre-board again and backed the headsails. Taking her time, Aunt Effie brought down his mizzen mast with a shot from Humpty, and blew away his rudder with one from Dumpty.

Then a peculiar thing happened. The pirate captain popped to the surface, and we all thought we heard him cry, "I love you, Euphemia!" but Aunt Effie howled like a hurricane through her speaking-trumpet and drowned his voice.

"Fancy you forgetting Rangi's Reef," she stormed. "And don't you dare call me that name again!"

We swabbed out Humpty and Dumpty, closed their ports, and turned back on course under ordinary canvas.

"What's the pirate captain's name?" asked Lizzie.

"Strange," said Aunt Effie, "but when he stood on the bowsprit, I thought his profile looked remarkably like that of the Maori chief, the one who signed the Treaty of Waharoa."

"I hope you didn't have any children by that marriage," said Daisy.

"Here's a tin of Brasso." Aunt Effie tossed it to her. "I

want to see both those chasers so shiny you can see your face in them."

Later, when Daisy came aft with the striped Brasso tin and the polishing rags, Aunt Effie said to her, "Turn your head around. Let's see your profile. Yes, I think you must be descended from Rangi. You've got his nose, as well as his cheek, Daisy. You can take these bits of canvas, and a needle and palm, and skip up and sew patches over the cannonball holes in the mizzen topsail. Make a seamanlike job of them or I'll keelhaul you."

For a dreadful moment, we waited for Daisy to tell Aunt Effie she couldn't keelhaul her because scows don't have keels. But before she could open her mouth, there was a huge explosion. Much louder than our guns, or the pirate's. A seagull got such a fright it lost its grip on the air, and fell upside down into the sea. We watched as it tried to fly underwater, then swam out of the side of a wave with a silly look on its face. High in the mizzen rigging, Daisy squawked. We sailed on, still hearing the distant booming, watching a column of black smoke to the south-west.

About a week after Aunt Effie wrecked the pirate on Rangi's Reef, we were making south under full sail. We'd had our early morning swim around the scow, holystoned the decks, polished the brass, and eaten a lump of salt junk for breakfast. We'd had our mid-morning swim around the scow, wiped down the brightwork, checked the parbuckling chains on our cargo of kauri logs, and had smoked snapper on toast for morning tea. We'd had our midday swim around the scow, and were looking forward to a lunch of roast pork crackling when Aunt Effie screeched at Peter, "Port your helm!" But since we were running with the centreboard up, the *Margery Daw* wouldn't come around: she made leeway instead.

One moment we were surging along, a white bone in our teeth. The next, the headsails flapped, the main, and the mizzen, and the topsails hung lifeless. The jaws groaned and creaked as the booms swung to and fro.

"We're going to need all our wild pork and smoked fish," said Aunt Effie. "We've run into the Horse Latitudes."

"Good!" said Lizzie. "Where are the sea horses?"

But the sea was still and silent. Neither a neigh nor a ripple. As we watched, a weed sprouted on its surface. Then another. The leaves interlocked and spread until the *Margery Daw* was held in their grip.

"Tarnation!" said Aunt Effie. "Sargassum weed!"

"Language!" said Daisy who disapproved of swearing. "Is that bad?" she asked. Daisy liked to look on the dark side of things.

"It looks as if the Horse Latitudes have moved south, the Doldrums have moved north, and they've both joined up with the Sargasso Sea. I've never known a ship trapped in the sargassum weed to escape. For all I know we might be somewhere near the Equator."

"In the Hauraki Gulf?" asked Daisy. She was good at geography, so we all looked at Aunt Effie.

"It might not be what they learn youse kids at school," Aunt Effie told her, "but the Gulf's bigger than most people think and changes shape when it wants to. One year when I was a girl, it stretched from the Tropic of Cancer to the South Pole. South of the Happy Jacks it froze over and we spent all winter skating with walruses."

"Walruses!" exclaimed Daisy in a disbelieving voice.

"Some people think of walruses as cumbersome beasts, but put them on skates and they dance very lightly, considering their size. Because of the intense cold and the weight of icicles on its arms, the Southern Cross hung much lower than usual that winter, and we danced on skates in the starlight: Captain Flash, Samuel – the profligate missionary, Chief Rangi, and I. They were all three elegant dancers: Captain Flash did a very creditable mazurka, but not even he could compete with the walruses when it came to the waltz and the foxtrot."

As she spoke of dancing on skates over the frozen Gulf, we shivered with cold, huddled together, and woke wrapped in eiderdowns on the foot of Aunt Effie's enormous bed.

Note: *"Here she goes again. Tressel, log-reef, bonnet, water-sail, wing and wing, palm, keelhaul, holystone, brightwork, parbuckle, Sargasso. I sometimes wonder if Aunt Effie herself knows what these words mean...."* —Daisy.

Chapter Twelve

Crossing the Equator

We hung on to the eiderdown, felt for the floor with our toes, and a big rough voice said, "Watch out for the Bugaboo!" Jessie and Jared were the smallest, but they beat the rest of us downstairs.

As we finished pruning the asparagus trees at the back door, Aunt Effie joined us. The rest of that day we spent raking and turning the grass as she scythed the tennis court, the front lawn, and began on the paddocks closed up for hay.

Several days later, the grass dry enough, we built a haystack in the orchard, one on the tennis court, and a couple on the front lawn. Aunt Effie showed us how to keep the sides straight, how not to stick your hayfork through your foot, and how to thatch the stacks with reeds. Half-a-dozen we built beside the barn looked like a village of cottages at the foot of a castle. A huge heap of leftover hay we forked into the barn.

To our surprise, Aunt Effie had insisted on building all the stacks on top of big konakis.

"What for?" asked Lizzie.

"You never know." Aunt Effie looked wise and wouldn't say any more.

"I want to jump on the haystacks!" Jessie complained.

"Well, you can't," said Daisy in her sensible voice.

"Why not?"

"Because Aunt Effie said so."

"Why not?"

"Because she said we'll make holes in the thatch, let in the rain, and ruin the hay."

"I don't care!" said Jessie, and Casey said she wanted to jump on the hay, too. And just then we heard Aunt Effie calling: "Daisy-Mabel-Johnny-Flossie-Lynda-Stan-Howard-Marge-Stuart! Peter-Marie-Colleen-Alwyn-Bryce-Jack! Ann-Jazz-Becky-Jane-Isaac-David-Victor! Casey-Lizzie-Jared-Jess!"

We ran and shinned up the dwangs and studs to where Aunt Effie stood in the rafters of the barn. "If you want to jump in the hay, jump down there," she said.

We looked down on the huge heap of hay, sniffed its lovely dry summery smell, joined hands, and jumped. When we didn't land on anything, Daisy shrieked, "We missed it!" We kept falling, Daisy still shrieking until, instead of smelling summery hay, we sniffed rotting weed and slimy creatures. Then our feet were landing on something that gave way, lifted under us, and gave way again. We were back on the gently rising and falling deck of the *Margery Daw*, still trapped in the Sargasso Sea.

It was too hot to think about roast pork crackling for lunch. We rigged awnings and lay gasping in their shade.

Aunt Effie rationed the drinking water and filled an eye-dropper from which she gave us one small drop each. "That's your lot, hearties!" she said cheerfully. "Until tomorrow."

The sails slatted, the sargassum weed heaved, and slimy things ran across its surface. We kept the decks wet, swilling buckets of water across them. When a breeze came, we tightened the sheets, but the sails fell empty again. "It does that in the Doldrums," Aunt Effie said.

Toad and mouse-fishes wriggled under the leaves of the weed. Daisy saw a yellow and black banded sea snake and spent two days sitting on the foremast cap till she had to come down to go to the toilet. At first the dogs were excited and tried to catch the little crabs that lived under the weeds, but soon sprawled in the shade of the awning, their tongues hanging out. Lizzie tried hanging out her tongue, but said it made her even hotter.

Three times a day, Aunt Effie gave us another drop of water, and we held it in our mouths as long as possible before swallowing. We didn't feel like eating anything.

When a storm burst, we rigged the mainsail and the mizzen to catch the rainwater. Unfortunately, the dried salt on the sails made it too brackish to drink.

One day Aunt Effie shook the eye-dropper and said there was nothing left in it. When we cried, she said, "We'll just to have to do a rain dance."

"That's a pagan superstition," said Daisy disapprovingly. "I'm not sure the minister at home would approve." But the rest of us followed Aunt Effie shuffling in a circle on the foredeck. We clapped our hands over our mouths and chanted: "Wah! Wah! Wah!" We danced backwards. We danced widdershins. And we begged for the Great Juju in the Sky to send rain.

When it thundered out of a clear sky, Daisy gave a yelp. "Now you've done it!" she cried and pulled her dress over her head. A black cloud appeared. Lightning cut a jagged hole, and rain poured through it in a waterfall. We tipped back our heads, opened our mouths, and heard our dry innards fill up like bottles gurgling to the top. The barrels lashed under the booms filled with sweet water. The dogs lapped it off the deck. That night we had pork crackling for tea, all except Daisy who wouldn't drink the water because we'd got it by behaving like a lot of ignorant savages. But still the wind didn't blow.

Phantom ships drifted past, caught in the sargassum weed for centuries. Skeletons clattered from side to side of their decks as the sullen heave of the Doldrums lifted and dropped the weed. "All dead of scurvy, plague, and yellow-jack!" said Aunt Effie. "Too late to help them. Best hold our noses and keep our distance."

She mixed our water with lime juice and wiggled our teeth with her fingers. "One of the signs of scurvy:" Aunt Effie said, "when your teeth start dropping out."

A ghost ship sailed past close on our port side one night, her sails drawing even though ours hung lifeless. A few nights later she sailed back down our starboard side, but again we couldn't feel any wind.

"The *Flying Dutchman*," Aunt Effie said. "Cursed to sail the seas for ever. Even in the Doldrums, he has to keep sailing."

"What did he do to get cursed?" asked Casey.

"Better not ask," said Aunt Effie. A spectral figure on the deck of the *Flying Dutchman* turned to look at us but, to our horror, it had no eyes. We ducked and hid under the bulwarks until he'd disappeared astern. Afterwards, we saw the paintwork along our starboard side was scorched....

The sea got smellier each day. Snakes and other slimy things lay on their backs and bubbled and hissed. Huge round heads lifted the weed and goggled from under its leaves. Alwyn told Daisy he'd seen a sea-vampire with long teeth, and each night she lashed herself high in the rigging, scared to go to sleep in case it crawled aboard and sucked her blood.

Several times each day we felt a light air and scampered, setting the sails. They filled for about five minutes, and the wind fell again. The weed closed about us, and we heard a thousand slimy voices chuckling and making swallowing noises: "Gollop! Gollop!"

When a giant sea serpent swam alongside, we shinned up the rigging, scrambling over each other to be highest. But the sea serpent lifted its horned head higher than our topmasts and sniffed us. It snorted, spat, and wriggled away across the seething water.

"I don't think it liked your smell," said Aunt Effie, "or it would have plucked you off the rigging and eaten you like ripe apples."

One morning there was a strong stink of fish. Braying like foghorns and climbing up the bobstay and over the bows, an old man and an old woman clambered

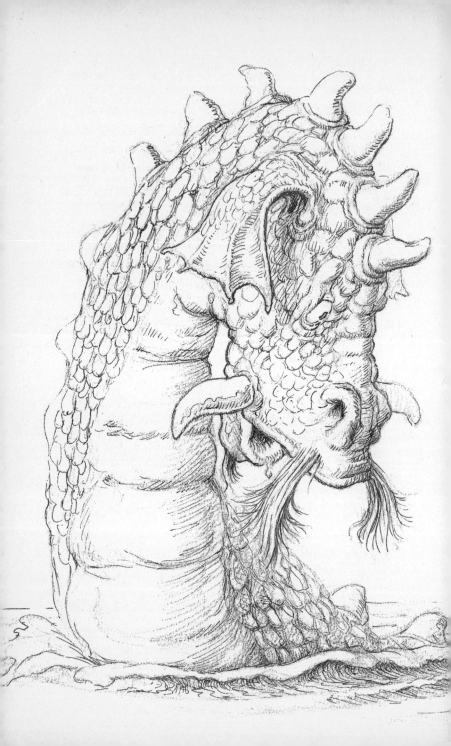

aboard. Apart from seaweed hanging off their heads and shoulders, they were naked.

"Tsk! Tsk! Tsk!" said Daisy, and rushed forward with a couple of blankets in one hand and the other over her eyes.

"Slubberdegullion!" the old woman said and dragged Daisy up to the old man, who sat himself on an upturned bucket and daubed tar on her nose. When Daisy complained, he painted her face, flicked his fingers and tied her hair in a thousand knots. They shaved Lizzie with thick soap and a cutlass, and Lizzie kept very still in case they cut off her nose. They washed Casey's hair with a bottle of something that smelled like Old Puckeroo. They gave Jared a haircut with a huge pair of

wooden scissors that tugged and made him squeal. And they tattooed Jessie from head to toe with black mud from the bottom of the sea.

King Neptune – for that's who he was – chased the rest of us up the rigging with a trident and down the other side where we fell headfirst into a barrel of mutton birds preserved in ancient whale oil. When the dogs smelled us, they ran away howling. Then we had to bow and kiss the king and queen's feet. Their toes were webbed, their legs covered in green scales.

"I declare you all proper and able seamen of my watery kingdom!" said King Neptune, and they dived over the side and swam along a straight black line towards the sunset. Queen Neptune swam, half-sitting in the water, a very dignified backstroke, but King Neptune porpoised along doing a rather showy butterfly stroke, puffing loudly, and calling to the queen to keep up. Dolphins curvetted, snorted, and splashed about them.

"Look!" said Jessie. One dolphin leapt higher than all the others, and across the water came the thrilling cry of a horse's neigh. Then another, and another. "Sea horses!" cried Jessie. "See how high they jump!" Rainbows shimmered in the spray they flung. As King Neptune's procession disappeared into the setting sun, we held our breath and heard one last distant neigh.

"I've never seen the Horse Latitudes so mixed up with the Doldrums and the Sargasso Sea before," said Aunt Effie, "but you can never tell what you'll see in the Hauraki Gulf."

"What's the black line?" asked Lizzie.

"The Equator. If we can just get across it, we'll be in for some good sailing."

We heard a conversational rustle from the sea. Catspaws rippled towards us. A fine breeze filled the sails. We pulled up the centre-board, and there was a bump as The *Margery Daw* sailed over the straight black line of the Equator. The centre-board hummed as we dropped it, and the cutwater ripped the sea apart with a noise like blue satin tearing. "The South-East Trade Wind!" said Aunt Effie. "With any luck it'll carry us right into Auckland."

"What if we don't have any luck?" asked Daisy, looking on the dark side as usual, but Aunt Effie was busy pulling in a blue and silver kingfish that we ate for breakfast.

Nothing beats sailing in the Trades! Each morning we got up early, swam twice around the scow, holystoned the decks, polished the brass, and had breakfast of flying fish that had landed on the deck overnight. At midmorning we swam around the scow three times, wiped down the brightwork, checked the parbuckling chains on our cargo of kauri logs, and drank our issue of grog laced with lime juice to stop our noses and ears dropping off with the scurvy. At midday, Aunt Effie taught us to shoot the sun with a sextant, find our position, and mark it on the chart. Then we swam twice around the scow and lunched on roast pork crackling.

At night we watched the pointers move around the Southern Cross. The huge stars swung to and fro so low that sometimes they scraped the paint off the tips of the topmasts. We got sick of having to climb up and repaint them each morning. The moon was so bright, the canvas sails turned to curved sheets of silver. We swayed in our hammocks, wriggled our shoulders, and listened to the salt crackling on our skin.

"If we ate ourselves, would we taste like pork crackling?" asked Lizzie.

"Ask Aunt Effie," said Daisy. "She should know. After all, she ate the cabin boy!" But nobody took any notice of Daisy now. Even Boris, Brutus, Nero, Caligula, Kaiser, and Genghis stopped growling and, so long as the Trade Wind blew, they didn't bite her.

Aunt Effie said we had to keep up with our school work and taught us navigation, physics, and personal hygiene. Navigation was steering the *Margery Daw* by the stars at night and the sun by day. Physics was trimming the sails, raising and lowering the centre-board, and making the best of the wind.

"Never jam a scow on the wind," Aunt Effie reminded us. "Ease her off a point or two and she'll gain in speed what she loses in leeway."

Personal hygiene was swimming around the scow as often as we could, gargling with salt water, and sloshing down the decks after the dogs. Boris, Brutus, Nero, Caligula, Kaiser, and Genghis loved swimming around the scow with us, but they didn't know much about personal hygiene on deck.

"We'll have to remember to make a dirt box for them," said Aunt Effie. "Dogs like a bit of dirt." Kaiser whined at her. "Of course!" Aunt Effie said to him. "And a bit of grass to chew now and then – just to keep you healthy."

It must have been the thought of green grass beneath our bare feet that did it. We closed our eyes and thought of home. The vast blue Gulf, the curved sails, the regular cotton-ball clouds of the South-East Trade Wind all disappeared. We opened our eyes and found we were sitting in the top of the big pear tree back in the orchard, picking the last of the fruit. It was autumn, and the dogs were pawing and whining, snuffling at something under a stump. "Yowl!" Kaiser cried and rubbed his soft nose along the ground.

"Serves you right!" said Aunt Effie. "If I've told you once, I've told you a thousand times not to go pushing your snout into the hedgehog's nest when he's trying to go to sleep for winter." She pushed together the straw, wisps of hay, and twigs that covered the hole under the stump. "Poor old hedgepig," she said. "He tries to hibernate but never quite gets there before Kaiser goes waking him up."

"What's hibernate?" asked Lizzie.

"I'll show you, when it gets colder," Aunt Effie promised.

Note: *"Dwang, widdershins, juju, and slubber-degullion! I ask you, what sort of words are they? Does Aunt Effie just make up words to confuse the little ones?"* —Daisy.

Chapter Thirteen

How Rangitoto Island Got its Name

Winter coming on, we dug the potatoes and stored them in clamps. We filled the bins of sand in the barn with parsnips, carrots, turnips. We sliced and salted runner beans in the big brown jars, picked the last of the peaches and quinces, and pulped the last of the tomatoes. As their vines withered, we rolled the pumpkins, green, grey, gold, and orange, down to the barn.

"Stand them in the sun and turn them round a bit each day, Casey-Lizzie-Jared-Jessie," said Aunt Effie. "It hardens their skins for keeping. Think of the soup we'll have this winter!"

"Eeugh!" Jessie wrinkled her nose.

We spent several days picking the maize and filling the cribs while the chooks scurried and pecked the bright grains under our feet. We killed twenty fat shrieking pigs and rubbed the hams with salt. Each morning, yesterday's salt had turned to brine, and we drained it off, rubbed more salt into the flesh, and saltpetre beside the

made were so small, he had to crouch over them so the only part of him that got warm was his pot belly! Everybody else went cold."

We sledged the baskets of grapes on the konaki, and tipped them into the big wooden vat. We scrubbed our feet and legs in the creek, climbed into the vat, and trampled and squashed the grapes. By the time Aunt Effie ran the juice off into barrels we were red all over.

"What a shame you're not old enough to drink wine!" she said. "Maybe you can have just a taste of mulled wine this winter!" But Daisy clicked her tongue and went, "Tsk! Tsk! Tsk!"

We set rows and rows of apples – the keepers – on the floor of the attic above the barn. The dusty air filled with their fragrance and made us dizzy. Between us we carried the clothes-baskets filled with windfalls and big cider apples into the pressing shed. Casey and Lizzie led the old white horse round and round so he turned the stone wheel in its circular gutter and squashed the apples to pulp. We shovelled it on to the flat table and turned the big handle that brought down the press. Juice ran into the barrels together with flattened wasps, bees, twigs, and butterflies.

"Ooh!" we said, "we're not going to drink that stuff!" But, as the juice worked, the wasps and other rubbish came out the bung-hole in the top and only pure golden cider was left in the barrel.

"A pity you said you don't want to drink it," said Aunt Effie.

The cheese room was filled with great round cheeses

ripening, orange, yellow, and red. "Think of the cheese on toast we'll eat this winter," we told Daisy who didn't like cheese.

We wiped the scythes and sickles and secateurs with wisps of straw, and oiled and hung them in the shed. While Peter and Marie spent the morning hammering and sawing in the workshop, the rest of us spent it jumping on the hay in the end of the barn. We squashed it down so far, Aunt Effie remembered a leftover heap in the bull paddock, and we filled the barn up to the rafters again.

One day when there was a frosty nip in the air, and Aunt Effie said somebody reckoned they'd seen a skiff of snow on top of the Kaimais, we heard her calling us: "Daisy-Mabel-Johnny-Flossie-Lynda-Stan-Howard-Marge-Stuart! Peter-Marie-Colleen-Alwyn-Bryce-Jack! Ann-Jazz-Becky-Jane-Isaac-David-Victor! Casey-Lizzie-Jared-Jess!"

We ran into one of the sheds off the barn and found her by the huge fermenting barrels filled with grape juice. "Has it turned into wine?" we cried.

"Don't lean too far or sniff too hard or you'll fall in and drown drunk," Aunt Effie said. "Just stick your nose over the edge and let it fill your nostrils."

At the heady scent, we went cross-eyed, fell on our backs, stuck out our tongues, and kicked our legs in the air, pretending to be drunk. All but Daisy, who didn't think it was funny.

"Jam one ear against the side of the barrel and close your eyes," said Aunt Effie. We jostled for places, stuck one ear against the side of the barrel, and heard the rustle and conversation of fermentation.

"It's singing to itself," said Jessie, and Daisy pushed herself in to hear, too.

We were silent. We listened and smelled something sharper in the air. Not so sweet and musty now. More like salt. And the rustling, whispering, fermenting voices changed to a regular splash, a running sound like water falling.

"Open your eyes!" ordered a gruff voice.

We woke in diamond-sharp sunshine, staring down through the netting spread under the bowsprit of the *Margery Daw*. Dolphins rode the bow wave. Lizzie reached over to pat one, fell in, and the dolphin caught her between its teeth and tossed her back on deck. For the next couple of days, she kept limping and showing everyone the scratch on one leg.

Each day as we sailed towards Auckland, the same booming we'd heard before got louder and closer. The dogs pricked their ears and sniffed the air, and we began to smell something, not the salty smell we were used to, but something ever so slightly rotten.

Aunt Effie looked at our hair. "You haven't got nits, have you?" She went through our hair with the kooti comb, looked closely at its teeth, but said we were all right. Then she'd pick us up and sniff us as we ran by, and she'd put us down again and say, "No. It isn't you."

"The dogs," said Daisy. "It's their personal hygiene."

"It's not them," said Aunt Effie. "Not now they've got the dirt boxes Peter and Marie made them. Are you sure you had a bath last Saturday night?" she asked Daisy. But it wasn't that sort of smell.

One night, the sky was overcast, and we saw a red glow spread across the bottom of the clouds.

"Is it the Doldrums again?" whispered Jared. "Remember the thunder and rain?"

"If it's Rangi the pirate," said Lizzie, "let's shift one of our guns to the stern so we can fire backwards this time."

"That Rangi will be busy rebuilding his scow from the thrashing it took," said Aunt Effie. "No, it's something bigger than guns. And that smell's stronger, too. I think I know what it is."

"What? What?"

"Well, you know how Dunedin has trouble with the climate?"

"Yes! Yes!" we all said.

"And you all know how Christchurch has trouble with the smog?"

"Yes! Yes!"

"And how Wellington has trouble with earthquakes?"

"Yes! Yes!"

"Well, what does Auckland have?" asked Aunt Effie.

"Trouble with volcanoes!" we all shouted and ran up the rigging with the telescope.

Aunt Effie steered through the Tiri Channel and headed towards the North Shore. East, the sea smoked and boiled. Black water or mud slurped up and something stuck a smoking snout out of the sea.

"A dragon!" said Jessie. "Look, you can see its ears!"

Alwyn jumped into the ratlines and bellowed the

noise he thought dragons make. The smoking snout went under and came up again, higher this time, and it groaned. Alwyn hid behind Aunt Effie, stuck out his head and groaned back. Rumbling, grumbling, spitting, hiccuping, and burping, the new volcano rose and slid tongues of lava down its hardening sides into the sea that hissed, bubbled, and turned black. It stunk!

"Sulphur and brimstone!" Aunt Effie said.

The westerly wind carried the smoke and showers of ash towards Motutapu Island. We didn't want to get too near so lifted the centre-board and skimmed along just off Long Bay, Torbay, and Browns Bay. As we ghosted past Mairangi Bay, the water steamed. Off Castor Bay we caught a feed of snapper over our starboard side and cooked it in the boiling sea over the port side.

The volcano's cone now stood high above the sea. What Alwyn and Jessie had thought was a dragon's snout and ears was now a central peak surrounded by several smaller knobs.

"The likeness is quite extraordinary," said Aunt Effie. "See, the top of the cone looks remarkably like Rangi's great toe, and the smaller peaks below are his lesser toes.

"We didn't have a chance to look at his feet," said Daisy rather unnecessarily.

Aunt Effie ignored her. "I think we'll name it after him," she said. And as every Aucklander knows, the name stuck, though the spelling changed a bit.

Aunt Effie was feeling bad about our schooling again, and she tried to use the birth of Rangitoto Island, to interest us in geology.

"Notice," she said, as we swept along past Milford and Takapuna beaches, "the old solidified flow of rock from Lake Pupuke." She pointed at Black Rock.

"There's no volcano there," said Victor.

"There is!" said Aunt Effie. "A caldera-type volcano. Lake Pupuke is its crater. That's why fresh water comes out of the sand at Black Rock. And there, astonishingly close –" she gestured at Rangitoto, "– there is a cone-type volcano building itself up with successive layers of lava and coarse debris."

"You sound like Daisy," Lizzie told her, and Aunt Effie grinned.

"Daisy-Mabel-Johnny-Flossie-Lynda-Stan-Howard-Marge-Stuart! Peter-Marie-Colleen-Alwyn-Bryce-Jack! Ann-Jazz-Becky-Jane-Isaac-David-Victor! Casey-Lizzie-Jared-Jess!" she shouted. "Duck!"

The sea lashed as a rattle of stones from Rangitoto fell on deck of the *Margery Daw*. We got under the bulwarks just in time, but the stones dinged on the tin basin Aunt Effie put over her head as she stood at the wheel. Thinking he had bitten him, Brutus bit Boris, Caligula bit Nero, and Genghis bit Kaiser. We swept the deck and were relieved that Aunt Effie's lesson in volcanism had ended, but we were also pleased to know how Rangitoto Island got its name.

Note: *"How can I make a glossary if she doesn't use any difficult words?"* —Daisy.

Chapter Fourteen

Harbour Stow

Under a full press of sails, and with a bone in her teeth, the *Margery Daw* stormed on to the Waitemata Harbour. Fifty guns thundered a salute from North Head, and Humpty and Dumpty replied, "Pop! Pop!" The Mayor stood on top of the Ferry Buildings and waved her gold chain around her head. The aircraft carriers at Devonport dipped their ensigns. So many Aucklanders ran to wave and cheer that the end of Queens Wharf bent under their weight. That's why people still slip off it today.

Banners and bunting flew as we sailed under the huge wooden bridge that used to join Queen Street and Devonport. People have forgotten about it now because it burned down in the Great Fire of Auckland in 1951, the night the police fought the wharfies.

Aunt Effie steered between a Short Sunderland flying boat taking off for Sydney, and a couple of scows carrying horses to South Africa for the Boer War. We knew our sails had been spotted because the great log-booms were opening below the Kauri Timber Company mill in Freemans Bay.

"When I was a girl," said Aunt Effie, dodging a couple of canoes carrying peaches, kumaras, and raffle tickets from the Thames, "Auckland was as flat as Christchurch. Then the volcanoes popped up: Mount Wellington, Mount Hobson, Mount St John, Mount Smart, Mount Eden, Mount Roskill and Mount Albert. All named after the old Queen's former lovers, except Mount Victorious which she named after herself of course."

"Why did she name Mount Victorious after herself?" asked Lizzie.

"Look at her statue in Albert Park," Aunt Effie said. "Queen Victorious and Mount Victorious are the same shape."

A Devonport ferry tried to cut across our bows. "Steam gives way to sail!" Aunt Effie bellowed, "and don't you forget it!"

The ferry captain ran out of his wheelhouse, swept off his cap, and bowed. "Sorry, Euph–" he began to shout in return, but Aunt Effie bawled through her speaking-trumpet so we didn't hear the rest of it.

"Instead of being very flat–" she turned and shouted at us. "Sorry," she said, and took the speaking trumpet away from her mouth. "Instead of being very flat," she said in her normal voice, "Auckland was now very steep. Roads and fences now sloped where the volcanoes had bent them up and down. You can still see where the city council had to put steps into some footpaths. And quite a few people had to build staircases when they woke and found their houses were now two-storeyed.

"The Auckland Museum used to be a one-storey building at the bottom of Grafton Road, but it was lifted up on top of the volcano where it now stands. Suddenly it had several storeys, and that's why they had to prop up the roof in front with those big pillars."

As she talked, we dropped the topsails and swung out our heavy lifting gear. Off Freemans Bay, we backed the headsails, scandalised the main and mizzen, and let go the parbuckling chains on the port side. Because there were no bulwarks amidships, the outer logs stirred like elephants waking and rolled overboard. As the *Margery Daw* rolled to starboard, we let go the chains and the logs splashed off that side. To and fro she rolled as we jacked and swung and unchained the logs so they rumbled and trundled and thundered into the water. The K.T.C. men rowed out and worked them inside the booms.

We watched our first log go up the chute on an elevator and on to a platform that carried it into the breaking-down saws. Their steel teeth spun and whined. At the shriek from the first cut, we stuck our fingers in our ears.

"That was our kauri tree shrieking!" Jessie said. She burst into tears, and the saws screeched again.

"It's what happened to almost all the kauris," Aunt Effie said, and we cried and wished we hadn't cut down ours.

"It's progress," said Daisy. "Think of the money!"

Aunt Effie nodded. "The Kauri Timber Company's owned in Melbourne, so most of the money from the kauris went over there. Very little stayed in New Zealand."

"It's no use crying over spilt milk," said Daisy. "The man in the mill told me our kauri tree will build a whole street of houses. Ow!" We were all pleased when Caligula bit her behind.

We cried for the kauri tree as we picked up our moorings in St Marys Bay. We cried as we put a harbour stow on the sails so the rain didn't get in and rot them. When Daisy smiled and pointed at a fresh-sawn stack of kauri planks outside the K.T.C. mill, we cried all the louder.

We cried so much Aunt Effie had us up all night pumping out the bilges so we didn't put the lee chine under and tip upside down at our moorings. Next morning we sailed on top of the tide up to the head of the harbour. Aunt Effie kept looking south, sniffing the air, and saying, "I can smell snow."

Without our load of kauri logs, we skimmed across the mudflats, centre-board up. Off Hobsonville, we saw a couple of moored flying boats. As we passed Herald Island, a steam-driven triplane took off from Whenuapai. We watched the coal smoke it left behind as we slipped past Lukas Creek and ghosted up to Riverhead. Under topsails only, we worked our way several days up the Kumeu River. The mudflats sprouted mangrove roots like a miniature forest. When we tried drinking the water, and found the corners of our mouths didn't turn up, we knew we'd reached tidal limits.

We made everything shipshape for winter, greasing the metal work, lifting the centre-board out of its case, striking the topmasts, running in the jib-boom, taking down the rigging, and hoisting the rudder on deck. We set up shear-legs and struck down both masts. We lashed tarpaulins over the hatch covers and the wheel. We polished and greased Humpty and Dumpty and stitched them inside their green canvas covers like dead sailors with a pyramid of cannon-balls at their feet. We crawled through the bilges with buckets of salt, scattering handfuls under the overhangs and into the limber holes because it's fresh water that rots wood. And then we warped and kedged the *Margery Daw* downstream into a mud berth amongst mangroves and reeds.

"She'll lie here hidden, safe and snug in the mud for winter," said Aunt Effie. "One thing the fresh water will do: it'll kill all the weed on her bottom."

Without masts or rigging, just a hulk moored to deadmen sunk in the mud, it no longer looked like our lovely scow. Casey, Lizzie, Jared, and Jessie stood up in the dinghy to wave one last goodbye. "Sit!" ordered Aunt Effie. "You'll have us over!"

As we came down the harbour on the outgoing tide and passed the K.T.C. mill we set our faces towards Northcote so we couldn't see what they had done to our kauri tree.

"Daisy-Mabel-Johnny-Flossie-Lynda-Stan-Howard-Marge-Stuart! Peter-Marie-Colleen-Alwyn-Bryce-Jack! Ann-Jazz-Becky-Jane-Isaac-David-Victor-Casey-Lizzie-Jared-Jess! Watch where you're going!"

We backed our oars. The long boom of a schooner-rigged scow swung over our heads. We glimpsed the name on her stern, then we were going down her starboard side. Her crew hung over the bulwarks, chewing tobacco, swigging kegs of rum, and calling out unpleasant things about our rowing.

"Ahoy, the dinghy!" one of them hailed. "Who's that sheila, the one with the silly hat?"

Since we were arriving in Auckland, Daisy had insisted on wearing a hat and gloves. Unfortunately, the hat had ostrich plumes and did make her look a bit silly. She shouted back, "Don't you dare call me a sheila!" and did a little dance of rage before we pulled her down. The ostrich plumes nodded and made her look even sillier.

The crew of the rakish scow guffawed and rolled their glass eyes. They clapped their hooks together – they had no hands – and we could hear the clatter of wooden peglegs on the deck as they followed us, spitting tobacco juice till the sea turned brown, and we slipped under their bowsprit and headed in towards Freemans Bay.

"Did you see the name of that scow?" Victor whispered.

"Yes!" we all whispered back.

Before we could shut her up, Daisy said in her loudest carrying voice, "I'm sure I've seen the captain of that scow before. Wasn't he the same man who was the skipper of the Devonport Ferry?"

"Nonsense!" said Aunt Effie. "Caligula-Nero-Brutus-Kaiser-Genghis-Boris, leave Daisy alone!"

The rest of us looked at each other. We had read the scow's name written across her stern. And we had all seen her captain run out on her bowsprit, take off his hat, and make a sweeping bow to Aunt Effie. He shouted something, but the K.T.C. mill blew its whistle for knock-off time.

"Greasies!" Victor said, "I smell greasies!"

"Say fish and chips," Daisy corrected him. "It sounds more dignified."

But we were all saying, "Greasies!" and turning our heads to sniff the wind coming off Freemans Bay.

"That scow–" Daisy started to say, but Aunt Effie interrupted her.

"Where we're floating now will be dry land in a hundred years' time," she said as we rowed sniffing under the sterns of a couple of other scows. We landed and pulled the dinghy well up the beach and turned it over.

"That scow–" Daisy began again, but Aunt Effie went on in a loud voice. "They'll dredge the harbour and dump the sludge in here. Once they've reclaimed the bay, they'll plant it in grass and call it Victoria Park," she said. "Years later they'll build a flyover for the harbour bridge motorway on concrete legs away above us."

We didn't know what Aunt Effie was talking about. Even Lizzie didn't ask what was a flyover.

"That scow–" Daisy tried again.

"Four of the concrete legs that will hold up the flyover, where it crosses Victoria Park, won't be concrete at all. They're the masts of two old scows they'll bury when they reclaim the park. But people won't notice because they'll be painted to look like concrete."

We weren't listening to Aunt Effie because it sounded too like a history lesson, besides we were all too busy sniffing and following our noses and the smell of greasies up the beach and across the road. The roar and the stink of beer and smoke coming out the door of the Robbie

Burns pub knocked us over. Daisy stuck her head in the door and shouted, "Wine is a mocker, and strong drink is raging!" The men inside stared at Daisy's ostrich plumes as we got to our feet, staggered on, and picked up the smell of greasies again.

"You're in luck," said Greasy Mick in his fish shop at the foot of College Hill. "I dug the spuds for the chips this morning and caught the fish off the beach just before you landed. They're so fresh, the fillets are still flapping. Lie down, you dogs!" He smacked a couple with his fish slice. "What'll you have, snapper or terakihi?"

"Both!" said Aunt Effie. We left the oars with Greasy Mick, and he promised to keep an eye on our dinghy.

He brought our fish and chips down to the beach in a wheelbarrow. He tipped the huge newspaper-wrapped parcel on to the sand, took the lid off a kerosene tin of tomato sauce, and said, "Bon appetit!"

When we stared at him, he explained, "Foreign lingo for: 'Enjoy your tucker!'"

We lay in a circle and gorged ourselves. A thousand seagulls joined us but burned their beaks trying to swallow the chips hot and had to hold their heads under water. Ann always felt sorry for seagulls, so she gave them her last piece of fish. One by one we rolled on our backs in the sand and groaned that we couldn't eat any more.

"I'm as full as a tick myself," said Aunt Effie. We drank bottles of ginger beer with marbles stoppers in their necks instead of corks. And we gasped and burped while Daisy went, "Tsk! Tsk! Tsk!"

"It says here in the editorial it's going to be the worst

winter in several hundred years." Aunt Effie was reading from the *Herald* the greasies had been wrapped in. "We'd better get home and see the house and the barn are all right." She turned over the page. "The rural reporter says it's going to be so cold, stock might have to be brought inside. If that's the case, we'll have to do something about the hay as well."

"That scow we nearly bumped into," said Daisy speaking quickly in her loudest voice, the ostrich plumes nodding on her silly hat. "Did you notice it's painted black, and it's schooner-rigged? And it's called the *Lady Euphemia*!" None of us was near enough to stop her. "I heard what the captain called out. I'm sure I heard him saying, 'I love you, Eu–'"

Aunt Effie snapped her false teeth and rattled and shook the newspaper. The noise of it crumpling and crackling made us stick our fingers into our ears and close our eyes. When we opened them again, we were sitting on the end of Aunt Effie's enormous bed, our mouths and lips still greasy. We tried to lick the last brown crumbs of fried fish batter off the eiderdown, but the dogs beat us with their longer tongues.

"Who's going to boil the billy and make a brew of tea to wash the grease out of our gullets?" asked Aunt Effie.

"We will!" Without thinking, we all jumped to the floor. There was a terrible chewing noise, a sort of "Gollop! Gollop!" as if something waiting under the bed was licking its lips and swallowing.

"Watch out for the Bugaboo!" said a gruff voice. We saw bony fingers reach from under Aunt Effie's enormous bed and clutch cold around Daisy's ankles. She kicked and shrieked, and her ostrich-plumed hat fell off, but we dragged her away by her hair and ran screaming and skipping downstairs.

Note: *"I'm often scandalised by Aunt Effie's behaviour. But what does it mean to scandalise sails? Look up the glossary at the back of the book."* —Daisy.

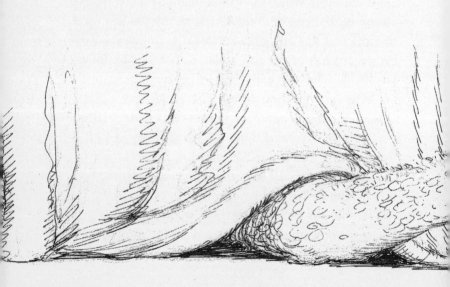

Chapter Fifteen

To Bring Back the Spring

We lifted the turnips and swedes, and sledged load after load to the barn. We moved the stock, cleaning up the last of the summer grass. The sheep grew round as balls of wool and rolled nibbling from one paddock to another. The cows munched until their hips disappeared under swathes of fat, then stood drowsing in the autumn sun, chewing their cud and swishing flies with their tails. The pigs guzzled and scoffed and gobbled, and grew double chins like hippopotamuses. The girths wouldn't meet around the horses' bellies, and the donkeys had the squinty look that comes from having a fat face. They all grew thicker coats.

"Daisy-Mabel-Johnny-Flossie-Lynda-Stan-Howard-Marge-Stuart! Peter-Marie-Colleen-Alwyn-Bryce-Jack! Ann-Jazz-Becky-Jane-Isaac-David-Victor-Casey-Lizzie-Jared-Jess!" We climbed the ladder and stood in a row on the roof while Aunt Effie tied a bowline under our arms, and lowered us down the chimney. We swept it clean with tea-tree brooms, and popped out of the fireplace in the kitchen, black all over but for grinning white teeth.

After a bath we put on our pyjamas and coughed until Aunt Effie gave us each a liquorice strap and a bagful of bull's-eyes to clear the soot out of our throats. Then we lit the first fire of winter, put on the old horse blankets we used for dressing gowns, ran outside, and looked up. The chimney puffed a perfect smoke ring and wrote our names in black letters upon the cold white sky. Instead of smoke, the chimney from Aunt Effie's bedroom blew bubbles.

"She's at that pipe of hers again," said Daisy disagreeably.

Lizzie pointed at the Kaimais. "What's all that white?"

"Snow," Peter said. "Look, it's thick on Mount Te Aroha!"

"What's snow?"

"Atmospheric moisture in the form of ice crystals," Daisy told her crisply in her penetrating voice.

"Can you eat it?" Lizzie asked, but Aunt Effie called our names. "Come and listen to the wireless," she said. "It says there are icebergs off Mercury Bay!"

"Will the *Margery Daw* be all right?" asked Jessie.

"Snug as a bug in a rug in her mud berth," said Aunt Effie, and we all laughed. The idea – icebergs in Auckland Harbour!

Then the wireless said they were soon going to have to stop broadcasting for winter. "The air is getting too cold for the radio waves to pass through it without freezing and falling on people's heads," said the announcer.

"That's really cold!" said Aunt Effie. "Time to bring the animals inside."

For once, Daisy's strong, carrying voice was useful. She called the cows, sheep, horses, pigs, donkeys, geese, chooks, turkeys, bantams, and ducks, and they came flying, trotting, waddling, cantering, rolling, and mooching into the barn. The bulls wouldn't wait for us to open their gate, but smashed down their strong fence and galloped, tossing their long horns, winking their wicked little eyes, and kicking lumps of mud over their heads. They bellowed threats at Alwyn for teasing them, but we knew they were secretly pleased to be coming inside from the cold. Only one foolish sheep kept trying to get out of the barn and run away.

"The gluttonous wolves which come down from the Vast Untrodden Ureweras in hard winters will almost certainly eat that one," said Aunt Effie.

Each animal had its own stall with its name on a brass plate over the door, a manger of hay, and a trough of fresh water. They could stick their heads over the walls and talk to each other, or keep to themselves if they wished. The sheep crowded together in the skillions to one side of the main barn, all of them but the foolish one. There was plenty of room for the poultry, though the sly geese sneaked into the turkeys' enclosure and pooped all over their floor. That night, the turkeys roosted on the rafters above the geese and got their own back. They only stopped squabbling when Daisy told them off.

"They listen to her," said Alwyn, "because she looks

a bit like a goose herself."

When the big gander hissed and flapped his wings and tried to scare her, Daisy told him, "Pride cometh before a fall." He was quiet after that, just hissing when her back was turned.

As snow got lower on the Kaimais, Aunt Effie led the way to the haystacks, each of us riding one of the draught horses, the chains and swingletrees slung up over their withers. Aunt Effie felt among the hay at the bottom of the stacks, found the ends of the konakis they were built upon, and hooked on the swingletrees. We gidduped the draught horses, they heaved forward, the traces tightened and, one after another, the haystacks swayed and sledged in a huge procession.

The last one slid into the barn on its konaki just before dark. The horses rolled on their backs before padding on giant feathered hooves into their stalls and the oats and chaff waiting in their mangers. We rubbed their noses. "Good horses!" we told them, and they shook their heads, snorted, and blew chaff like a storm.

That night, Aunt Effie stuck a red-hot poker into a bottle of wine, and threw in a handful of spices. "Mulled wine!" she said. "Good for what ails you." She gave us each a sip from her mug. When our noses stopped sneezing, and our eyes stopped running, we drank cider mixed with cocoa, honey, and hot milk, and that went down better. Aunt Effie finished the bottle of mulled wine on her own, with Daisy going, "Tsk! Tsk! Tsk!" and muttering, "Wine is a mocker." Daisy always had an apt quotation from the Bible for anything enjoyable.

After tea, we sprawled on cushions in front of the huge fireplace. "Tell us a story?" asked Jessie, and Aunt Effie said, "Once upon a time, when my great-grand-mother was a young girl, there was a cold winter. Snow was so deep, they dug a tunnel to the barn, but it collapsed on top of my great-great-grandfather, and they had to pull him out by his feet. It took them two days, but, fortunately, he was used to holding his breath that long while he emptied the old dunnies."

"Why did he hold his breath to empty the dunnies?" asked Lizzie.

"They stunk something terrible," said Aunt Effie. "You've no idea what a pleasure it is to have proper toilets with flushing water!

"After being pulled out of the snow by his feet for two days, my great-great-grandfather couldn't get shoes long enough to fit him. He had to go barefoot the rest of his life and suffered terribly from chilblains in winter and stone bruises in summer.

"He had to cut a door through the back wall of the house and into the barn to feed the animals." Aunt Effie stopped and thought. "I wonder if that door is still there?" She shook her head and said, "The snow was so deep that winter, they couldn't get to school."

"What?" said Daisy in a shocked voice.

"The snow was so deep, the Hopuruahine school had to close."

"How did your great-grandmother learn?" demanded Daisy.

Aunt Effie smiled. "Everybody in Waharoa did their

lessons through the Underground Correspondence School."

"What's the Underground Correspondence School?" asked Lizzie.

"It's a postal school in Wellington that sends lessons to all the children through pipes underground. It only works when it's too cold for the schools to stay open."

"Mr Jones won't close the school," Daisy said. "Anyway, he hasn't even opened it yet."

In those days, schools closed in summer and opened only in winter. The rest of us had been going for ages, but Casey, Lizzie, Jared, and Jessie were going to start that winter for the first time.

Aunt Effie told us the rest of the story about her great-grandmother doing her lessons by the Underground Correspondence School, and we piggybacked the little ones to bed and tumbled asleep ourselves.

Each day the snow crept lower down the Kaimais. We tied hay around our bare feet to stop the chilblains, and ran through the frost to feed the animals and poultry. When our toes got too cold, we raced each other to the freshest cow muck and stood in it till they tingled warm again. We screeched and made so much noise, the cows wouldn't let down their milk, and Peter told us to knock it off.

We mucked out the stock and tossed in fresh straw. The bulls were very particular and stood on their hind feet to make it easier for us to clean out their stalls. The horses were even cleverer: they stood on one foot only – and hopped out of the way as we swept and shovelled.

Only the one foolish sheep tried to get out each time we opened the barn door.

Lizzie lost her temper and told it, "The gluttonous wolves will eat you, when they come down from the Vast Untrodden Ureweras!" But the foolish sheep went, "Baa!" at her and ran away again.

Noses running, bare feet stinging, turning up our toes against the frost, we danced back to the house where Aunt Effie ladled out porridge from the camp oven. We covered it with brown sugar, poured on jugs of yellow cream, and dug our porridge into islands with creeks like the one where the *Margery Daw* was snug as a bug in a rug in her mud berth. Then Aunt Effie gave us bacon and eggs and toast and home-made marmalade and jam and boiling-hot cocoa sweetened with dark, secret, tea-tree honey from the beehive in the barn roof.

"It's getting too cold to let the fires go out at night," said Aunt Effie. We used timber-jacks and gun-tackles to roll and slide and hoist backlogs into all the fireplaces, big enough to keep smouldering away for months.

Before lighting the fire in the kitchen one morning, Marie and Peter slid out the bars on the doors in both sides of the great chimney. We held them wide-open, and Aunt Effie drove twenty draught horses, the muscles standing out separate on their huge shoulders and shining rumps as they strained, hooves battering the stone floor, through one door, across the fireplace, and out the other. Whinnying relief, they looked around while we unhooked the whole tree trunk they'd dragged in for a backlog.

"Black maire," said Aunt Effie. "It should last us till spring."

It took all of us, turning the handles on our timber-jacks, to roll the dark-timbered trunk against the back of the vast stone fireplace. We slammed and barred the chimney-side doors. When we returned from putting the horses away, Aunt Effie brought back the shovel of embers she'd kept – because the fire in the kitchen must never go out – and we all knelt and watched Daisy and Jessie, the oldest and youngest of us, light a fire of apple prunings against the great backlog. The house filled with the fragrance of apple-blossom so we all looked outside, thinking spring had come.

"Why will it last till spring?" asked Lizzie.

"Black maire," said Aunt Effie again. "So dense and heavy, it burns hot and slow, without so much as a spark, and never goes out. All you need to do is throw some apple prunings against it each morning."

"Why apple prunings?" asked Lizzie.

We sniffed to show Lizzie we all knew the answer, but Aunt Effie replied, "To bring back the spring," as heavy-footed she tramped slowly upstairs.

Note: *"Bowline, skillion, swingletree, withers. That must be just about the last of them."* —Daisy.

Chapter Sixteen

A Message from the Prime Minister

One afternoon, Lizzie asked, "Where's Aunt Effie?" and we realised we hadn't seen her for several weeks. We searched the barn, the plantations, and the patch of bush down the back of the farm. We looked in all the paddocks. We scoured the swamp, all the drains and creeks. We hunted through all the sheds.

"Aunt Effie!" Daisy called in her carrying voice, but there was no reply.

We found Aunt Effie in bed, a sou'wester tied under her chin, an oilskin coat around her shoulders, her feet on a stone hot-water bottle. She wore her green canvas pyjamas. An empty bottle of Old Puckeroo Winter Tonic and Strengthening Remedy lay beside her pillow, and she snored steadily. The dogs on the foot of her enormous bed raised their heads and stared at us.

"Aunt Effie's hibernating," said Boris.

"You can talk!" said Jessie.

"What's hibernating?" asked Lizzie.

"Of course we can talk! Aunt Effie's gone to sleep for winter. Like a bear."

"Who'll look after us?" asked Daisy.

"You'll be all right," said Brutus, and Caligula added, "You've got all that food stored. And you've got plenty to do, looking after the animals. School starts next Monday. Aunt Effie said make sure and be there by nine o'clock before Mr Jones finishes ringing the bell."

Kaiser, Genghis, and Nero nodded, dropped their heavy heads between their paws. Brutus and Caligula did the same. Boris looked at us and said, "She'll be right!" He dropped his head, and they all began to snore in time with Aunt Effie.

As we tramped downstairs, Lizzie said, "None of us thought of the Bugaboo."

"I think we're safe from him," said Marie.

"Why?"

"Because the Bugaboo is hibernating, too. I heard him snoring under the bed."

Down in the kitchen, Peter turned on the wireless. It was very faint. He turned it up as loud as it would go. A long way away, a tiny voice said: "This is Radio Station 2YA, Wellington, of the National Broadcasting Service of Waharoa. Here is a message from the Prime Minister."

There was some static. We pressed closer to the wireless. Somebody struck a couple of notes on a piano. "Stand up!" Daisy cried, and the piano played "God Save Queen Victorious" while Jazz sobbed noisily. Royal occasions always brought out a melancholy side to his personality.

There was a hiss and the sound of a door slamming. "That's the wind. It's always blowing in Wellington," Peter told us.

"This is the Prime Minister speaking," said a big strong voice.

"She sounds like a man," Jared said.

"She's supposed to be a woman," Lizzie told him. "She just looks like a man."

The Prime Minister talked on and on about God and the Opposition. We drifted away, but scampered back to the wireless when we heard our names called.

"Daisy-Mabel-Johnny-Flossie-Lynda-Stan-Howard-Marge-Stuart-Peter-Marie-Colleen-Alwyn-Bryce-Jack-Ann-Jazz-Becky-Jane-Isaac-David-Victor-Casey-Lizzie-Jared-Jess!" said the Prime Minister's mannish voice in one breath.

We stared at each other.

"Here is a special message to all the nephews and nieces of Aunt Euphemia! Keep yourselves warm! Look after the animals! Go to school and learn to read! Do your homework! If it snows, watch out for gluttonous wolves, grizzled bears, and man-eating rhinoceroses coming down from the Vast Untrodden Ureweras! Above all, make sure you put a good breakfast beside Aunt Euphemia's bed before she wakes up!" There was a pause. "Behave yourselves!" There was another pause, and we heard the Prime Minister begin to snore.

"She's hibernating, too," said Jared.

Alwyn grunted and snored back at the wireless. "What if the Prime Minister hears you?" asked Daisy.

"She called her The Name We Dare Not Say!" Marie said. "Twice!" We listened and heard a growl come down the stairs from Aunt Effie's bedroom.

The wireless played "God Defend Waharoa", hiccuped, and was silent. Then it came alive, played the first two lines of "Now is the Hour", and stopped with a bang and a shriek as if somebody had slammed the lid on the pianist's fingers. We held our breath and stared at the brown cloth above the dial where the sound seemed to come from, but there was nothing more. Peter turned the wireless off to save the batteries, and Jessie began to cry.

Somewhere outside there was a long howl: "Ooowhooooo!" as if a wild animal was sad, cold, and very hungry.

"Just the wind in the chimney," said Peter, but we all stood at the door with a lantern while he and Marie ran and made sure the barn doors were barred.

"One of the sheep is missing," they shouted. "The foolish one. It must have got out of the barn!"

We joined hands and searched the orchard and the garden. We searched the bull paddock. There were no signs of tracks in the light snow. It was quite dark as we searched around the barn and the house one last time. "Ooowhooooo!" we heard again, closer this time.

Screaming we ran inside, slammed the door, and listened at the foot of the stairs for Aunt Effie's snore. Outside, the wild animal howled again. "Ooowhooooo!" and we heard a sheep baa.

"Do something somebody!" Daisy wept. The little ones stared at her.

Peter barred the door and drew the curtains across the windows. "It's the foolish sheep that was always running away." He looked at us. "It's not worth risking our lives for it."

Outside we heard "Ooowhooooo! Baa! Ooowhooooo!" There was another "Baa!" and then the chewing and swallowing noises the Bugaboo sometimes made under Aunt Effie's enormous bed.

"We can't do anything about it now," said Peter.

Before Marie could stick her hand over his mouth, Alwyn threw back his head and went, "Ooowhooooo!"

"OOOWHOOOOOH!" went the wild animal, much louder and closer. We huddled together. Marie hissed at Alwyn, "For goodness' sake!" The wild animal bumped and scratched against the door. We heard snuffling and huffing and "Gollop! Gollop!" noises.

"It's licking its lips," someone whispered.

"It's looking through the keyhole!" Daisy screamed, but Peter pulled a thick curtain across the door.

"Tomorrow," he said calmly, "we'll screw steel shutters over the doors and windows."

"Poor sheep!" said Lizzie. Casey, Jared, and Jessie cried with her.

"We'll all feel better when we've had something to eat," said Marie. "It's teatime!" But none of us felt like eating when we found it was mutton stew.

As usual, Daisy had the last word. "'There is a time for everything,'" she said with gloomy cheerfulness. "A time to eat, and a time to be eaten. Winter time starts tomorrow. And school opens at nine o'clock. And about time, too. Oh!" she exclaimed, "I am looking forward to doing my homework!"

Upstairs, Aunt Effie snored.

The End

Daisy's Glossary

"*Only sissies use glossaries.*" —Aunt Effie.

"*A glossary is a very useful thing! So there!*"—Daisy.

"*Back in the old days when we were kids, our money was pounds, shillings, and pence. We measured distances in miles, yards, feet, and inches. We weighed things in tons, pounds, and ounces. Everything was much better then!*" —Aunt Effie.

"*It's wicked to look back and say things were better then. We must look forward and hope for the best! So there!*" —Daisy.

aft behind, near the stern
auger a large hand-turned wood drill
backstay a supporting rope from the mast aft
baulk a heavy, squared length of timber
bigamist "*Some poor devil with more than one husband or wife....*"—Aunt Effie.
bilges the area where water collects inside the bottom of a vessel
block a ship's pulley
blockhead ("*Daisy!*" —Aunt Effie.)

blunderbuss a short gun with a big mouth (*"Like Daisy!"* —Aunt Effie.)

bogie a four-wheeled tramway trolley which carries one end of a log

bonnet an extra strip of canvas laced to a sail to catch more wind

bookau debris of leaves, gum, cones, twigs, and bark around the foot of a kauri; used to make dams watertight

bookie someone who takes bets illegally

boom 1. The spar along the bottom of a sail; 2. Logs chained across to catch and hold other logs (3. *"A noise Daisy makes."* —Aunt Effie.)

boom-jaws jaws holding the boom to the mast (*"Daisy's mouth when she's booming."* —Aunt Effie.)

bosun an officer who looks after the ship and her gear

bower an anchor carried at a ship's bow

bowline a useful knot for sailors, and for Aunt Effie when she lowers us down the chimney

bowsprit a spar that sticks out from the bows

brightwork varnished parts of a ship

broad-axe 1. a wide-headed axe for squaring and flattening timber (2. *"One of my favourite weapons."* —Aunt Effie.)

bulwarks the sides of a ship above the deck

cable a rope or chain to the anchor

cable tiers the coiled and stored cable

camp oven a large, round, iron pot with a tight-fitting lid, for cooking over an open fire or in the ashes

cap a round wooden piece to protect the top of a mast

caulk to stuff the cracks between planks with watertight material

centre-board a moveable keel that lifts and drops inside the centre-case

centre-case a long narrow box that holds a centre-board

chain-plate a strong plate on the ship's side to which the shrouds are fixed

chaser a cannon in the bows or stern, useful when chasing or being chased (*"What Aunt Effie sometimes calls a drink of Old Puckeroo."* —Lizzie.)

chine the angle where the bottom of the hull meets the side

chock a wedge to stop something moving

chock-a-block blocks on a tackle tightened right up against each other

coffer-dam a temporary dam to turn a creek aside while a bigger dam is built

coir rope a floating rope made from the fibrous outer husk of the coconut

con to direct a ship

Crimean shirt a blue or grey flannel shirt worn outside the trousers like a bush shirt

curry-comb a comb for grooming horses

cutwater the part of a ship's stem that divides the water

deadeye a round three-holed block for tightening shrouds (*"A deadeye is what's under a pirate's eye-patch."* —Jessie.)

deadman a post dug into the ground and used for anchorage or leverage

dog an iron spike with a loop to take a chain

doldrums an area with no winds

drag-tooth a curved tooth that clears the cut of sawdust

drive to send logs down a river

dwang a bit of wood nailed between studs in a building (*"The noise a shanghai makes when it backfires."* —Jared.)

epaulette a shoulder trimming to show rank (*"Captain*

Flash's epaulettes were very showy and made him look so handsome!" —Aunt Effie.)

fathom six feet; about 1.8 metres

flitch a length sawed from a log

flume the gap in the dam through which the logs were driven

fore ahead, near the bows

forestay a supporting rope from the foremast to the bowsprit

frames the ribs of a ship

freeboard the amount of a vessel above water
("When you don't have to pay on the Devonport ferry." —Casey.)

gudgeon a socket that the rudder pintle fits into; together they hold the rudder to the stern and let it turn

halberd a long pole ending in a spear and a battleaxe
("Another of my favourite weapons!" —Aunt Effie.)

halliard a rope for pulling a sail up or down

hawse-pipe a metal pipe in the bows, through which the anchor cable runs

headsails sails on the foremast or bowsprit

head sheets ropes controlling the headsails

helm ship's wheel or tiller

holystone sandstone used to scour the deck

hoodoo someone who brings bad luck

horse latitudes a belt of calms

jam on the wind to sail too close to the wind, when the scow loses way

jib-boom a spar that lengthens the bowsprit

juju a magical spirit

jumper stay a stay on the top of the masthead

kedge 1. a small anchor for hauling off after grounding;
2. to pull on the kedge anchor and so move the ship

keelhaul to punish someone by hauling them under the keel (*"What I'd like to do to some people!"* —Aunt Effie.)

ketch a two-masted vessel whose mizzen-mast is shorter than the mainmast and stepped ahead of the rudder post

knee a bent timber used in shipbuilding

konaki a horse-drawn sledge

kumara pit a storage hole for kumaras

lace-bark (also known as **ribbonwood**) a New Zealand tree with lacy bark useful for trimming hats or twisting into cord

lanyard a short rope

lee chine the chine on the side away from the wind

lee side the side away from the wind

leeboard a raising and lowering wooden board fixed to the side of a ship as a keel

leeway sideways drift

limber holes drainage holes which let bilge-water run to the pump

log-reef taking up the lower part of the mainsail to clear a cargo of logs

lugsail a four-cornered sail fixed to a yard that crosses the mast at an angle

Manila rope rope made from Manila hemp

maul a long-handled, wooden-headed hammer (*"Very useful in battle."* —Aunt Effie.)

mizzen-mast the mast nearest the stern

nikau a New Zealand palm

oakum caulking of fibres unravelled from old ropes soaked in tar (*"Not to be confused with old tars soaked in rum!"* —Aunt Effie.)

Old Furry Aunt Effie's favourite soup made from split peas, ham-bones and any old leftovers (*"It tastes like old horses' hooves!"* —Ann.)

Old Puckeroo Aunt Effie's favourite medicine (*"Wicked liquor."* —Daisy.)

overhangs places where you have to crawl below decks (*"A bit like a hangover."* —Aunt Effie.)

palm a leather protection you put on your hand when using a sail-maker's needle

parbuckle a rope or chain arranged for lifting heavy things

pawl a hinged catch that stops a wheel from turning backwards

pike a long pole with a spike (*"Useful for chasing slow people up the mast!"* —Aunt Effie.)

pike-pole a long pole used for shifting kauri logs in a drive

Pillars of Hercules the rocks either side of the entrance to the Mediterranean Sea – now called Gibraltar and Ceuta

pintle a vertical pivot for a rudder

pit-sawing sawing a log over a pit; the unfortunate man in the pit gets covered in sawdust (*"A form of punishment that should be used in schools!"* —Aunt Effie.)

port left side of a boat looking ahead (*"A lovely sweet wine."* —Aunt Effie. *"A sinful liquor."* —Daisy.)

possie place

quoin a wedge for raising and lowering a cannon barrel

rafters squared logs spiked to the main stringer of a dam and set into holes in the creek-bed. Planks were then spiked horizontally across the rafters to make the face of the dam.

ratlines a ladder of ropes fastened between the shrouds

recoil a cannon's jump backwards when fired

ricker a long, slender, straight tree trunk or pole

rito or **korito** the delicious heart of a nikau (*"Yummy!"* — Aunt Effie. *"You're not allowed to eat it!"* —Daisy.)

rolling road track made of smaller logs along which kauri
   logs were tumbled

rowlock a thing which keeps the oar in place

running rigging ropes that move, e.g., halliards

Sargasso Sea a place of confusion and uncertainty

scandalise to let sails hang so they don't work properly

schenam a creamy mixture of shell lime and whale oil,
   used to keep the teredo worm from eating scow hulls

schooner a very fast ship with sails rigged fore-
   and-aft ("*A very tall glass of beer.*" —Aunt Effie.)

scow a flat-bottomed sailing vessel built in New Zealand
   from 1873 to the 1920s for the coastal trade

shanghai a catapult

shear-legs a tripod of three poles fastened at the top and
   carrying tackle for raising and lowering heavy weights

sheet 1. a large anchor carried for an emergency; 2. a rope
   controlling a sail

shrouds supporting ropes from the masts to the chain-
   plates on the sides of the ship

sill the log across the bottom of the flume of a kauri dam

singe to burn the bristles off a pig

sinker a kauri log so full of gum it sinks ("*Daisy trying
   to swim after a meal.*" —Alwyn.)

skillion the lean-to part of a shed or barn

slow-match a wick or match kept burning without a flame
   ("*A very boring game of cricket.*" —Jazz.)

slubberdegullion a dirty fellow, a sloven

smoko morning or afternoon tea ("*Time for a swig of
   Yellow Jack!*" —Aunt Effie.)

snatch block a block with a hinged opening for inserting
   the bight or loop of a rope rather than its end

snipe to chop round the end of a log so it can be dragged
   easily

spar a pole used to hold sails and rigging

splice to join ropes (*"Splice the mainbrace! Yo-ho-ho, and a swig of Yellow Jack!"* —Aunt Effie.)

sprag to wound oneself on a piece of wire

standing rigging fixed ropes such as shrouds and stays

starboard right side of a boat looking ahead

Stockholm tar tar made from resinous pinewood and used in shipbuilding to protect wood and rope

strainer post a heavy fence-post stayed to take the strain of the wire

strike below to lower something into a ship's hold (*"There's some people I'd like to strike below!"* —Aunt Effie.)

strop a short strong rope for lifting things

sway to hoist

swingletree a bar to which a horse's traces are fixed; the swingletree itself is fixed to the wagon or load

tack to change the direction of a sailing ship

tackle ropes and blocks used to lift, move, and tighten things

tide-water booms logs chained across where fresh and salt water meet

tom a pole or log used to prop up the front of a kauri dam

topmast a mast attached on top of the lower mast

touch-hole a small hole in the breech of the cannon through which the charge is set off

tout a racehorse spy

trade wind a tropical wind that blows towards the equator

transom part of the stern

tressel a wooden device on the lower mast to support the topmast

tripping hook a metal hook that helps hold a dam gate closed

tripping rope the rope that trips a kauri driving dam

tripping-pole a pole that holds the tripping hook in place on a dam

trunnions round lugs that let a cannon pivot on its carriage

wad a disc of paper or cloth that holds the cannon-ball in the barrel

watersail an extra sail set below a studding sail in calms

weather side the side the wind blows against

weevil a biscuit-loving beetle

whare a hut

whim a winch or windlass like a capstan, used in the bush to haul logs and heavy loads, and sometimes set horizontally instead of vertically

widdershins anti-clockwise; against the direction of the sun

wing and wing with sails set out to each side; to sail goose-winged

withers a horse's shoulders

yard a long spar from which a square sail is hung

yard-arm either end of a ship's yard

yellow jack fever; also the name of one of Aunt Effie's wicked drinks (*"Yummy!"* —Aunt Effie.)

"Not everything in this glossary is true."
—Aunt Effie.

"Everything I say is always true! So there!"
—Daisy.